ROADSIDE VALENTINE

ROADSIDE
VALENTINE

◢◣◢◣◢◣

C.S. ADLER

MACMILLAN PUBLISHING COMPANY *New York*

For my editor, Phyllis Larkin,
whose perception, caring and conscientiousness
have nurtured my books well.

Macmillan Publishing Company,
a division of Macmillan, Inc.
866 Third Avenue, New York, N.Y. 10022
Collier Macmillan Canada, Inc.

Printed in the United States of America

10 9 8 7 6 5 4 3 2

LIBRARY OF CONGRESS CATALOGING IN PUBLICATION DATA

Adler, C. S. (Carole S.)
Roadside valentine.

Summary: Seventeen-year-old Jamie struggles for
love, independence, and the beginnings of maturity
during his senior year of high school.
I. Title.
PZ7.A26145Ro   1983   [Fic]   83-9394
ISBN 0-02-700350-7

ACKNOWLEDGMENTS

With thanks to Frank Cannizzo and Paul Hurteau
of the Niskayuna Schools Physical Education Department for their
help and expertise on the section of this book involved with men's
gymnastics.

As soon as Jamie got the idea, his spirits rose and the shadows in the empty apartment lost their power over him. He'd go out and buy a Christmas tree, the biggest he could find. They still had the box of ornaments his mother had cherished from her childhood. She'd left them behind along with everything else when she ran off with her Jamaican sailing captain eight years ago. The movers had stowed the box somewhere in the storeroom with all the other nonessentials from the old house. Jamie's father had said the huge old place was impractical for just the two of them, but Jamie had liked it. With its duck pond and the barn where cats were forever having kittens, he and his friends had never run out of things to do, and winters were cozy by the open fireplaces.

The white-walled and glass space of this efficient, modern condominium could never be cozy, but tonight, at least, when his father saw fit to leave his hospital patients to their own recovery, he would come home to the magic of colored lights

1

and shiny ornaments and the scent of evergreen. "Merry Christmas, Dad," Jamie would greet him and hand him his present—tapes of Bach and Brahms and Beethoven, the heavy music Dr. Jake Landes favored.

Jamie slung his physics text at the thick shag area rug and sprinted back out to his car in the parking lot behind their section of the large-windowed, gray wood townhouses. His balky, ten-year-old clunker started most easily while the engine was still warm. "Gotcha," he said aloud when it caught on the first try.

Now where had he seen Christmas trees for sale? Nothing along the county road between the pillared entrance to the condo complex and the high school. In the other direction, near the four corners where the shopping mall had been built, a gas station had a few trees for sale, but an even better possibility occurred to Jamie. Murphy's Tree Farm. He grinned. That made two good reasons to get a tree—to brighten up their apartment and to see Louisa Murphy.

In one of their recent brief exchanges in the halls of the high school, Louisa had mentioned that the old farm her family had just acquired had fields of Christmas trees. "You ought to buy from us this winter, Jamie," she had said.

"I would," he'd answered her regretfully, "but we never have a tree. Dad and I spend every Christmas in New Hampshire." He'd told her about the Staedlis, the Swiss couple who ran the ski lodge in New Hampshire. "They've practically adopted me. We even exchange presents." He had the run of their kitchen, and once when he was sick there Christmas week, Mrs. Staedli had brought him his meals in bed and fussed over him as if he were her child. How was Jamie to know his father had gotten bored with sliding down the same hills year after year and had decided not to go again? The best Jamie could do this year was send the Staedlis a greeting card and address it to "my Christmas family." He wondered if he'd ever see them again.

"You're old enough to vacation with your own friends," Jake had said, to justify not going to New Hampshire. Apparently he hadn't noticed that Jamie was in limbo as far as friends were concerned. He'd cut out his drinking buddies after he totaled the car last spring in his junior year, and no new friendships had ripened since. True, he'd had an invitation to share a chalet in Killington with some guys, but he didn't want to get drunk every night with them. Also, he didn't want to leave Jake alone for the holidays. Not that Jake would ever admit he needed his son's company. Sometimes Jamie wondered if the need was all in his own head. He hoped not. If Jake didn't need him, no one did.

Jamie wasn't sure about the directions to Louisa's new house, but it was out toward Charlton, so he headed west from the county road. Louisa would have signs posted. She was undoubtedly running the whole operation for her busy, working parents. Natural organizer that she was, she couldn't help running things. Although, now that he thought about it, her name was not at the head of as many groups at school as it used to be—class secretary and some community service corps weren't much for her. Where was all that dynamic energy of hers going? No way to find out in their sixty-second "How ya doing?" exchanges in the halls in school. It would be good to have a real talk with her for once. Louisa. He smiled to himself, thinking how shocked she'd be to know how often she starred in his daydreams. From her point of view, he was still the sad little kid she'd tried to take care of in fourth grade after his mother had left.

He drove past an old country tavern whose window was lit by a beer advertisement. Should he climb its rickety wooden porch and ask for directions? The sun slanted in, casting a melancholy half-light over the empty fields. They weren't yet decorated with snow, but rolled away on either side of the road in muted winter reds and tans and browns. A speckling of houses marked the edge of woods and weed-grown fields. The people here worked in the old industrial plants in the nearby city where the manufacture of big equipment was becoming increasingly uneconomical and fewer workers were employed each year. Their alternatives were to move away or open an antique shop or car repair business in the barn or a hair styling salon in the spare room—businesses as unprofitable as the now failing industries that had once drawn their Italian and Polish ancestors to the area.

Jamie spotted a sign for Murphy's Tree Farm on a telephone pole and another one on the side of an empty building. He followed the arrows to a hillside full of trimmed trees and an old, white-shingled farmhouse in need of paint. A shed with a fenced lot enclosed some cut trees. Louisa was there all right, her vividness in sharp contrast to the somber day. Just the sight of her shaking out the branches of a tree to display to a glum-faced man and woman made Jamie feel good. He parked and stood outside the fence, watching her.

She was a handsome girl, about five foot ten, with a strong-boned face and skin so creamy smooth he'd always longed to stroke it. Her blue eyes radiated life; even her dark red hair sprang from her head in an electric mass of waves. She didn't look as big anymore as in their fourth grade class picture where she stuck out in the back row as if she were everybody's elder sister. Jamie stuck out, too, in that picture because of the big sad eyes in his baby face.

"What's the matter, Jamie?" Louisa had kept asking him when he'd skulked around the playground refusing to participate in any games. She'd been the only one to notice how he shivered in the cold of his loss. Finally, her persistence had made him blurt out that his mother had left home.

"But don't tell anybody, okay?"

She swore she wouldn't, and she brought him an apple the next day and tried in little ways to take over the mothering he was missing. She'd urge him to change into his boots to go home when it snowed and whisper to him that he'd forgotten to zip his fly when he came out of the boys' room. She'd try to share her lunch with him when he showed up for field trips without any. He had resisted her out of pride, but nevertheless, he'd liked having somebody there who knew, somebody who was watching out for him.

By seventh grade he'd grown tall enough to reach her shoulder, but in other ways they were more different than ever. Louisa was class president, busy, popular, good at everything including sports. Jamie had already fallen into bad ways. He palled around with kids who excelled in negatives—not caring about marks or adult approval, intent on seeing how much they could get away with. Jamie's place among these troublemakers was insured because he always had money for cigarettes and beer or pot, and he was always willing to share. He'd invited Louisa to the seventh grade party on a dare.

"I'll go with you, Jamie," she had said, "if you promise you won't drink or smoke or anything that evening."

"What's the fun then?" he'd asked with stupid bravado.

"Just dancing and being at a party is fun."

"Not for me, it isn't," he'd bragged.

"Well, then," she'd said, "if that's the way you feel about it, I guess we can't go together." She'd bitten her lip and looked sorry, so purely beautiful with that flashing inner light she had that his heart had turned furry in his chest. But he hadn't known how to back down and do it her way. Instead, he had adored her from a distance all the rest of that year. She didn't tower over the other kids so much by then. The boy who did take her to the seventh grade party was taller than she was. Jamie had suffered intense humiliation that he was still short.

They were the same height now, he guessed, and he'd managed to kick all his bad habits, but Vince Brunelli was her boyfriend. No way could Jamie compete with a guy like Vince, a good-looking six footer, built like a football player and with enough brains so that he'd already been accepted at MIT for the next fall. An everything guy for an everything girl. No, it was foolish to imagine himself here for anything more than a tree and a little conversation with Louisa.

When she finished tying a rope around the six-foot-tall spruce and helping her customers lift it onto the car roof rack, Jamie stepped out from his observation post beside the shed where the row of branch-bound evergreen trees was leaning.

"Jamie!" she cried with her usual warmth as she turned from her departing customers to him. "How nice to see you."

"I'm here to buy the biggest Christmas tree you've got to sell," he said.

6

"You don't need the biggest. It's twelve feet tall. You'd have to cut it in half to get it into your house."

"Our living room has a cathedral ceiling."

"Oh, right, I forgot that you're rich." Louisa wrinkled her nose as she smiled at him. "Well, if you really want a giant, I'll be glad to sell you one. Who's going to help you set it up?"

"You?" Jamie dared to suggest.

"You've got to be kidding! I'll be lucky to get away from here at all tonight. Dad's supposed to relieve me after school, but he's got Christmas presents to buy first. My mother needs my help with the big dinner for tomorrow, and we've got to get our own tree up before we pick up my two older brothers at the airport. When you've got six kids in the family—"

"Watch out!" Jamie warned as a goat the size of a small pony came running right at them. He pulled Louisa out of the way. The goat tried to climb the trees propped against the shed, knocking half of them down in the process. Louisa shook loose from Jamie and reached for the halter on the goat's neck.

"Naaa!" he bleated, yellow eyes wide with alarm.

Two boys of about eight and ten stopped short right at the goat's heels as Jamie grabbed the halter on the other side of the big animal.

"He chewed it off himself this time, Louisa," the freckle-faced older boy claimed. He had Louisa's intense blue eyes. "We didn't untie him or nothing."

"How come you're always around when this goat gets in trouble, Jeff?" Louisa asked, implying she suspected a connection. "You go and call Mr. Kwallek, and Billy, you go get a rope from the garage."

7

The goat shook his horns at them and continued his nasal complaint. "I'm glad you think it's so funny," Louisa said to Jamie, who was laughing as he helped her ease the goat over to the fence post.

"Isn't it?" Jamie asked.

"I don't know," Louisa said. "When you live in a madhouse like mine, it's sometimes hard to tell." As soon as Billy brought her the rope, she tied the goat to the post with a quick double hitch.

"Were you two teasing him again or not?" Louisa asked Billy.

"We didn't do anything to him," Billy said quietly. "He just grabbed off Jeff's cap and ate it."

"The cap with the pompon I made him?" Louisa asked.

Billy nodded.

Louisa laughed. "I'll bet Jeff didn't resist too hard. He's been trying to get rid of that cap for a year."

"I like the one you knitted me," Billy assured her.

"Good, then you better not let him grab yours."

Billy backed away from the goat, who looked at them balefully out of one yellow eye, lowered his head and strained hard against the rope.

"Take it easy, fella. Nice goat. Hang in there," Jamie said and offered helpfully, "Want to chew on my down vest while you're waiting, or would you prefer my ski mittens? I'd offer you a finger, but I need all ten."

"Be careful, Jamie," Louisa said. "He might take you up on that."

An old man with a scraggly white beard and a family resemblance to the goat came hurrying across the road behind

Jeff. "I told you to keep them brothers of yours out of my yard. I'm gonna get the police on them for molesting my goat," the old man yelled at Louisa.

Louisa didn't quail. "I suspect your goat got loose because his rope is frayed and not because of my brothers, Mr. Kwallek."

"That's what *they* say. I saw them worrying this goat."

"If you saw them, how come you had to be called to come get your animal?" Louisa asked coolly.

In the face of her logic, the old man opened his mouth, shut it and retreated with his animal, muttering as he led him off.

"You told him good, Lou," Jeff said approvingly to his sister. "He's a liar."

"Jeff," Louisa scolded, "how many times do I have to warn you to keep off that cranky old man's property? You know he'll fill your pants with buckshot one of these days, and it'll be your own fault."

A slim young father and a small girl carrying a sheathed saw got out of a car and started up the hill. The man called over his shoulder, "Going up to cut that tree we tagged last week, Louisa." She waved them on, up the pasture road toward the first tree lot which was filled with turnip-shaped Scotch pines in neatly spaced rows. Next she sent her brothers off to the household chores they were supposed to be accomplishing. Then she thanked Jamie for his help with the goat.

"Anytime," he said. "It's been fun. You haven't changed a bit, Louisa, just extended your talents to goat wrestling and standing up to mean old men."

9

"Speaking of talents," she said, ignoring his compliment, "I was glad to see your name on the men's gymnastics team, Jamie. That's excellent."

"How come you looked at the list? I didn't think you were into gymnastics."

"I'm not, really, but I keep track of what my old friends are up to, and any sports involvement has to be good for you."

"You mean, better than the drinking and carousing I've been known for? Yes, I guess it is."

"Also better than fooling around with girls who don't have much sense," she said.

"You heard about last summer?" He was amazed. "Who told you about Ginny Baker and me?"

"She did," Louisa said. "She told me her father almost made you marry her. . . . Ginny's in my youth group at church."

"Small world," Jamie said. "Well, it didn't work out." He shrugged. He still missed the physical affection he'd had with Ginny, even though they never had much to say to each other.

As a result of that relationship, his father had called him a jackass and said only a fool would get himself married at sixteen. "That's me," Jamie had agreed, "a sixteen-year-old fool." But he had realized, nevertheless, that it wouldn't have been too satisfying to marry a girl to whom he couldn't even talk.

Now he summed it up for Louisa by saying, "About all Ginny and I had in common was that we both enjoyed hugging."

"Do you still miss your mother so much?" Louisa asked sympathetically, reading something he hadn't meant into his admission.

"At my age?" Jamie raised an eyebrow and tried to project his sexual maturity to set Louisa straight. "I'm not ten years old anymore, you know." As usual, he wished he were brawnier so that she'd be more impressed with him. Even though he was as tall as she was now, he looked slighter and probably weighed less.

"Well, anyway," she said, "it's a good thing you didn't marry Ginny. You're both too young. Now, tell me what kind of tree you want. We have plenty of nice Scotch pine, but they tend to be short and bushy. The balsam run tall, but they shed their needles fastest. Spruce is nice, but all we have left are in the field to the right, and it's getting awfully dark to see what's out there."

"Balsam should do fine," he said.

"You and your father celebrating Christmas alone?"

"Just the two of us." He gave her his most winsome smile and suggested, "Listen, if you can't help me set up the tree tonight, how about coming over sometime this week to see how I've managed?"

"I'm sure you'll manage without me just fine," she said as she walked to the trees, dark against the fence in the dimming light. She selected one and shook it out to show him just as the overhead light on the shed turned on automatically. "Big enough?" she asked.

It looked too big, but he claimed he could manage it. He recalled how he used to go without a drink of water after recess in first grade rather than suffer the indignity of letting

11

Louisa lift him up to reach the fountain in the hall. She always was there to offer the short kids a boost up.

Now, to show her how he'd grown, he gripped the tree trunk through the branches and tried to heave it on top of his car. The tree was so much heavier than he expected that he nearly fell with it. She leaped to help him. For an embarrassing moment, they wrestled for control, pulling against each other.

"You don't know how to do it," she said.

"You always were a bossy kid," he answered, feeling the blood flush his cheeks as he held on stubbornly.

"You're right," she said and let loose so fast he stumbled backward. "But not anymore. At least, I'm trying."

With grim determination, he got the top half of the spruce onto the car. He could have shoved the trunk the rest of the way and scratched his roof in the process. Instead, he smiled at Louisa. "Want to give me a hand now?"

"Sure." She stepped forward and together they finished the job.

"Thanks," he said.

"Oh, Jamie," she said on a strangely falling note, and then, "Why don't you stop by *my* house sometime this week and see our tree? After tomorrow, things should calm down around here."

"Really?" he asked. "You're inviting me? Hey, how about we go somewhere together, you and I? Skiing, skating? Want to go bowling or to a movie with me?"

"Wait, wait, hold it." She held up a hand to stop him. "All I had in mind was for you to come over and hang out with my brothers and sister and me if you felt like some company."

"Wouldn't Vince Brunelli mind?"

"Don't be silly," she said. "I can have my friends visit without worrying about Vince. He doesn't own me."

"He doesn't?" It was the best news he'd heard all day.

"Listen, it's no big deal. If you feel like dropping by, you're welcome." She smiled. "You know, I've always liked you."

"Really?"

He stood there in such a happy daze that she stirred impatiently and said, "If you're going to get this tree up before your father gets home, you'd better get going, don't you think?"

"Right." He paid her, roped the tree into place and said his farewell. "*Joyeux Noël*, Louisa. And *Skoal* and *Feliz Navidad*, also *L'Chaim*. I'll come by the day after Christmas."

"Have a merry one, you goof." She waved as she went off to take care of the young father who wanted to pay for the tree he'd cut. "Don't eat too much plum pudding."

He drove off feeling exuberant, imagining himself in the arcade where his favorite video games were assembled and Vince Brunelli as a blip on the screen coming at him. Pow! He punched Vince's blip right out of existence. So what if Vince was formidable competition! After all these years of admiring her at a distance, he, Jamie Raymark Landes, had at last been invited into her home. Now was his chance to win her affections. Lucky thing Dad had vetoed that annual vacation trip. Lucky thing Jamie had turned down the chalet with his old drinking buddies. His virtue and consideration for others were about to be rewarded. His season to be merry was here at last.

◄2►

IT WAS DARK by the time Jamie drove between the stumpy
brick pillars of the condominium complex and past the land-
scaped pond. The big-eyed windows of two apartments were
graced by Christmas trees, but they were fake and his was
real.

He parked and lugged the tree inside, leaving it next to the
front door on the slick, white vinyl tile of the entry hall while
he went to locate the steel stand and boxes of decorations.
He hated the rattle and click of emptiness in the apartment.
The glass tables with chrome legs and leather chairs that the
decorator had touted as masculine made the place look more
like an office than a home. No wonder Jake was grim, having
to return each night to this. Well, the tree would enliven the
place. Jamie remembered his mother saying, "Christmas trees
are the only part of the Christian religion your father appre-
ciates." She was Catholic while Jake was a Jew, at least by
birth.

"Was it the difference in religion that made you fall out of love with Dad?" Jamie had asked her on one of his annual visits to Jamaica before she had died in a car accident two years ago.

"Religion had nothing to do with it," she'd said. "I just couldn't stand your father anymore. He's such a grouch. Thank God you're not like him, Jamie. You take after me, you lucky dog." And she'd laughed.

She had been a vivacious woman, full of color and quirky ways. Jamie believed she had been happy with Thomas, her genial Jamaican. It had been hard sometimes to be glad for her happiness because he missed her so much, but he had tried.

"You'll have a better life with your father," she'd insisted when Jamie had begged her to take him with her. She'd lied, he knew, just to make herself feel less guilty for leaving him. "Jake needs you," she'd said, and Jamie had thought *that*, at least, might be true. Although his father didn't act much more unhappy than he had before she left. Jake used all his energy working on people's hearts sixty-plus hours a week— the most dedicated cardiologist in town. Work was Jake's therapy, work for the mind and some racquet ball and golf to keep the body in shape. What he did for his spirit, Jamie didn't know. Sometimes he suspected his father's emotions had atrophied and he was making it solely on brain power.

As for Jamie, during the first few years alone, he had struggled hard not to be depressed and had tried to soak up enough laughter and love and sunshine in his annual two weeks in Jamaica to help him survive the rest of the year up North. But without his mother around, he'd had no highs in the humdrum of daily living. He'd had to manufacture his own, and sometimes what he'd come up with had been bad.

Just as he finished attaching the colored lights to the tree which he'd set up in front of the picture window, the headlights of his father's Mercedes swept the circular driveway around the frozen pond. Hastily Jamie plugged in the lights so his father could be cheered by them as he sped past to the garage he rented behind the winter-stricken tennis courts. The living room was a mess now—green needles and the torn tissue paper that had cushioned the ornaments in the sectioned boxes were scattered everywhere. The front door opened just as Jamie hung a miniature sleigh full of tiny packages on the narrowest top branch of the tree.

"Merry Christmas, Dad," he called heartily. His father halted on the threshold of the living room and stared. His eyes, framed by thick eyebrows and heavy cheeks, were always hard to read, as unchanging as the smooth dark hair that never got mussed. He was a burly man and tall, as unlike Jamie as an oak to a sapling, more unlike. They could have been different species. Jamie had wide shoulders, but he was narrow from the chest down. Jake was massive all the way. Jamie would have chosen to look like his father, but failing that, he hoped someday to be like him, a man dedicated to helping others.

"Why'd you bother with a tree?" Jake asked.

"Like it, Dad?"

"It sure makes a mess in the living room."

"I'll clean it up. Doesn't it look nice?"

His father grunted. "You know, I made reservations for us at the club and they won't let you in without a jacket and a tie."

"I'll get dressed. Don't worry. . . . I guess you're really nuts about the tree, huh?"

Jake shrugged. "It's okay." The corners of his lips lifted in a shorthand smile. His mother had always said that making Jake laugh was harder than shelling coconuts. She'd been a lot better at it than Jamie was.

He had twenty minutes left to get dressed after he had cleared away some of the clutter of boxes and papers. Jake hated clutter. Jamie didn't know whether that was a leftover from the operating room with its sterile demands or whether it came from his European parents, whose personalities Jamie could only guess at from the dark landscapes of canals and mountains that hung in ornate gilded frames on the walls of their living room.

After the decorator had finished their bachelor pad off with huge modern paintings in blobs of black and brown and tan to match the colors of couch and rug, Jamie's father had called the paintings junk and replaced them with these landscapes inherited from his long-dead parents. Jamie didn't like the landscapes any better than the modernistic blobs, but when he said so, his father had asked him, "Since when did you become an art connoisseur?" Questions like that were unanswerable. The dark landscapes remained.

Instead of the sport jacket which he preferred, Jamie put on the three-piece suit with matching tie and shirt his father had given him for his birthday last April. Mrs. Donovan, Dad's receptionist, had taken Jamie shopping for the suit. The gift, which Jamie had been hard put to appreciate, had been her idea, but other than that she was a nice lady. Divorced, ordinary looking, but with a good figure. Jamie had considered what it would be like if his father ended up mar-

17

rying Mrs. Donovan and decided that pleasant, talkative lady would be a decided improvement in their lives, but Jake had never progressed beyond asking her to be his occasional companion to medical society social functions. The other women Jake had taken out to dinner or been introduced to at parties and dated briefly hadn't progressed any further in his affections, either, as far as Jamie could tell.

Jamie looked at his scuffed black leather dress shoes and decided to polish them. It was that or risk having Dad comment on their scruffiness. With a shoe in each hand, Jamie walked to the kitchen in his stockinged feet. His father was standing at the sink sipping his nightly shot of twelve-year-old Scotch. He kept the bottle, not in the bar in the living room which was supposed to be for the guests they never had, but in the counter under the sink where the cleaning lady had her detergents and other cleaners. Ever since Jamie swore off alcohol after wrapping his car around a telephone pole on his way home from a beer blast last spring, his father had been apologetic about his nightly drink.

"If you want me to keep you company," Jake had said, "I'll forgo it."

"You don't have to, Dad. It's me that can't handle it, not you."

"I find one shot relaxes me, but I don't need it," Jake had said. "If it bothers you, just tell me."

"Don't worry. You're not tempting me," Jamie had assured his father. It was, he had come to believe, more the conviviality of the drinking crowd that attracted him than the alcohol itself. He liked the initial high all right, but the aftereffects cost too much. As for his father, anything that relaxed him was something Jamie favored.

18

Jamie dug the shoeshine box out of the bottom of the broom closet.

"What are you doing?" Jake asked.

"Looks as if my shoes could use some touching up," Jamie said.

"You're going to polish shoes with your suit and shirt on? For God's sake, Jamie, when are you ever going to learn to do the dirty jobs before you get dressed?"

Jamie raised his arms in mock surrender. "Caught in the act," he said. "You got me, Dad. Go ahead—shoot."

Jake didn't smile, just shook his head and turned away. Jamie sighed. He couldn't risk getting shoe polish on his shirt cuffs. A few swipes of the brush would have to do. He was putting away the shoeshine box when his father called from the hall, "Hurry up. We're going to be late."

Jake was wearing his navy blue blazer with gray flannel slacks and the gold cufflinks he'd inherited from his father. While Jake was not stylish, he was a meticulous dresser, always polished looking. No matter how much care he took, Jamie never felt as seamless as his father looked dressed up.

"Somebody waiting for us?" Jamie asked.

"That's not the point. It's simple courtesy to be on time when you've reserved a table."

It had been Jake's suggestion that they eat out to celebrate Christmas Eve, Jamie reminded himself as he followed his father to the car. Give the man credit for good intentions. Jake slid automatically into the driver's seat of his silvery Mercedes, and Jamie took his place on the passenger side. A fragment of a daydream played in his head. Jamie would be gray haired and feeble with shaky hands, and his father, black hair turned to white, would turn to him and ask, "Do you want to drive, son?" Then Jamie would take the wheel with the proud knowledge that he'd grown up at last. No doubt he'd promptly drive the car into the nearest ditch and kill them both, but at least he'd die happy.

They turned onto Route 146 and drove past the run-down rabbitry, the local eyesore people complained about to no avail. Jamie always rooted silently for the disreputable fellow who owned the rabbitry when he heard people talk about what a disgrace it was. Jake had no opinion on the subject. He wasn't interested in much outside the hospital and his home. Narrow vision, his wife used to call it. "All he needs is disease, death and disaster," she had joked.

They passed the high school complex, set back amid athletic fields shared with the middle school and one of the four elementary schools of the district. Jake offered his usual conversation opener. "So how's it going in school?"

"Not bad. I got that report done for social studies and zapped the incomplete I got last quarter."

"About time. And what's your plan for this vacation?"

"Oh, not much. Fool around. Sleep late. Maybe pick up a few bucks filling in at the desk at the racquet club."

"You'd better complete those college applications you've got stacked on your desk. Procrastinate much longer and you're not going to get in anyplace next fall."

"I know, Dad."

In silence, they passed through town—the single store, fire station and post office that made a tight little knot tying the loose strands of country roads together. They turned onto a four-lane highway and drove across the bridge into the city where Jake had his office across from the hospital. Jake pre-

20

ferred silence and Jamie was fighting a downswing in his mood. Staying cheerful around his father was always a struggle. They passed the industrial sprawl that destroyed the beauty of the riverfront downtown, and drove on into the oldest section of Schenectady where refurbished houses dated back to pre-Revolutionary times and bore plaques attesting to their early Dutch owners.

The club was an ivy-covered stone cube across from the handsomest stone church in the city. Jamie's mother had always resented the club. "Symbol of male dominance," she'd complained. It still didn't allow women anywhere but in the dining room as guests of members.

Tonight the dining room was well populated. Jamie had thought most people would be at home on Christmas Eve. Maybe the elderly couples already seated didn't have any children to visit or had children who lived too far away. Jake's table was near an artificial white tree festooned with fake snow and white decorations. Their waiter informed Jake that his ticker was working fine now, thanks to Dr. Landes.

"Good, good," Jake said and ordered a bottle of wine and seafood appetizers.

When the waiter departed with their order, Jamie began digging for conversation. "Don't you hate artificial Christmas trees, Dad?"

"Not particularly." Jake took an olive and offered Jamie the relish dish.

"You didn't celebrate Christmas at all when you were a kid, did you?"

"Good Jews don't celebrate Christmas. My parents kept the Jewish holidays and went to temple every week. They sent me to Hebrew school and I was Bar Mitzvahed, but by the time I went off to Stanford, I'd given up the whole religious package, whatever its wrapping."

"I didn't know you were brought up religious."

"Certainly I was," Jake said.

"How come I wasn't?"

"Your mother and I couldn't agree on what religion to indoctrinate you in. We decided our best bet was to allow you to decide for yourself when you were old enough."

"How could I decide without knowing anything?"

"A good point. I guess you'll have to take courses in college." Jake chuckled as if that were funny. Jamie frowned, not seeing the humor but wary of inviting Jake's scorn by asking for an explanation.

"Do you feel like a Jew, Dad?"

"I not only feel like one, I am one—a nonobservant Jew, and when I die, I'd like you to get a rabbi to say a prayer over my dead body. There's a plot next to my parents' graves for me. They paid for it. You'll find all the instruction you'll need in the safe-deposit box. You know where the key is, don't you?"

Jamie gulped the rest of his wine in desperation. "Hey, Dad, Merry Christmas," he said.

"Sorry," Jake's eyes showed a twinkle. "But you asked . . . *L'Chaim!*" He held up his wine glass, and Jamie echoed the toast, holding up his empty glass. *"L'Chaim,"* to life.

"I still can't understand why you didn't accept that invitation to rent a chalet with your friends," Jake said.

"Those guys! They'll just booze it up every night, and like you said once, 'That's no way to treat the body you've got to live in the rest of your life.' "

22

Jake nodded. "I did say that, you're right." He let the subject drop.

The Alaskan king crab Jamie had ordered made a reddish log pile on his plate. He was picking the meat out of one of the long, narrow claws and wondering if he should ask for a doggie bag when he realized the conversation had gone dead again. It was likely to do that with Jake unless it got continuous feeding. "How's it going at the hospital?" Jamie asked. "Save any lives this week?"

"As a matter of fact, there's a danger of losing one, a twenty-seven-year-old man who's in congestive heart failure due to a heart valve defect. He's been doing poorly, and I want to go in and check on him tonight. You don't mind if I cut out on you early, do you?"

"Not for a reason as good as that," Jamie said.

"Got a party or something you can go to?"

"Don't worry, Dad. There's always the game room. Last week I ran four hours on one quarter at Pac Man. You should've seen me. And I could've gone longer except they closed the place on me."

"That's a hell of a way to spend your time, son."

"Yeah, but it's fun," Jamie said. "You ought to try it. It'd take your mind off things."

"I don't need diversion. What I need is more hours in the day to do what I have to get done."

"Yeah," Jamie said. He wished he had something in his life as important as his father's work.

Jamie was enjoying the club's famous chocolate mousse, a rich, creamy confection he couldn't pass up even though he was full of crab and salad, when a trustee of the hospital came over to wish his father a merry Christmas.

23

"You remember Dr. Edmunds, Jamie?"

"Sure. Merry Christmas, Dr. Edmunds. How's the doctoring going?"

"Not doing any now that I'm retired," the sharp-featured old man said, peering at Jamie as they shook hands. "Gone to pasture but not to seed yet, or so I hope. Jake, you and your son want to join me in the billiard room later this evening?"

"No, thank you, Owen. Got to get back to the hospital."

"Can't forget your patients even on Christmas Eve? Well, I'm not surprised. Your father's a credit to his profession, son. You going to follow in his footsteps?"

"I'd like to try, sir."

"That's the ticket. That's what I like to hear from the younger generation. You in college yet?"

"Next year."

"Next year. Well, well," Dr. Edmunds considered. "That won't leave you with any excuse, Jake. Once the boy's gone, you'll have time to run for office in the county medical society."

"Better wait on that," Jake said. "Jamie's college applications haven't gone in yet, and his academic record isn't likely to open any doors."

"Not the student you might be?" Dr. Edmunds asked Jamie with a forgiving smile.

"I have my ups and downs," Jamie said, embarrassed by this public exposure of his weakness.

"Lots of other stuff to keep you interested besides schoolwork at your age," Dr. Edmunds said. "Well I remember!" He patted Jamie on the back as if they shared a failing in common. "Enjoy your dinner," he said, "and if you need any recommendations for medical school, and I'm still alive, keep me in mind." He walked off slowly toward the coat-room.

"I didn't know they wanted you to be an officer in the county medical society. That's an honor, isn't it?" Jamie said tonelessly. He was still sore from his father's put-down.

"I told them I didn't have the time."

"Because of me?"

"Well, I used you as an excuse to say no."

Jamie wondered. Was that true or had his father really turned down the opportunity for his sake, so that he could spend the little free time he had with his son? Jake was shy about owning up to good motives. Yet he did do generous things—this dinner together tonight, the gift of another used car last year after Jamie quit drinking. Best to let himself think his father was doing it for his sake. Best to give the guy the benefit of the doubt, but it was hard to excuse all Jake's put-downs as no worse than symptoms of a sour disposition. The truth, Jamie knew deep in his heart, was that he wasn't the son his father would have chosen.

Jake dropped him off at the condominium and turned around to drive back to the hospital. Jamie went directly to the racquet club building past the tennis courts. There Pac Man and Missile Command and the newest computer game they had were waiting to suck him into another world of weird noises, flashing lights and the bottled tension of escape and kill. Only two tennis courts were lit and in use. The racquet ball courts, which his father preferred, were tucked away in the annex.

25

The high school kid at the desk looked up from his comic book when Jamie greeted him. Maury was his name. Jamie knew him from his pot-head days and was pretty sure the kid still got stoned regularly. A wormy-looking boy, Maury had the notable talent of sleeping through long, dull class lectures undetected.

"Got you working Christmas Eve, huh?" Jamie said.

"Yeah, they stuck it to me. Boss says you'll be filling in for us some this week?"

"Yeah, I figure I'll earn a few bucks toward my car insurance," Jamie said.

"Yeah, well, don't let them short you on the hours," Maury said. "They get their kicks out of shorting you if you let them."

"Okay, I'll watch it, thanks," Jamie said, and moved on as Maury yawned and looked back at the comic still in his hands.

The game room was nothing more than a converted utility room, and as usual, Jamie had it to himself. He slipped his quarter into the slot and waited to be absorbed into the moving blips of color and the eerie whine and clangor that simulated a space war. He should have gone skiing, he admitted to himself. It wouldn't have killed him to spend this one week drunk. And his father didn't really need him around for company. All Dr. Landes needed was his work, not a son who was just an ordinary slob of a kid dumb enough to think a Christmas tree was going to cheer up a guy who'd been Bar Mitzvahed.

⌐3¬

LOUISA FLUNG OPEN the door and hugged him. "Jamie, you're a lifesaver." Her greeting gave him an instant high. He came down only slightly when she explained, "Pops forgot the slides for his bird banding talk, and the boys are off looking for animal tracks in the woods. Someone has to stay here in case they come back. Would you, while I bring Pops his slides? I'll be back in half an hour."

"Sure, I'll hold the fort and keep the faith. In fact, give me another hug and I'll be your slave for life," he offered.

"I don't need a slave, just a temporary baby-sitter." She pulled on her blue quilted jacket and told him, "Make yourself at home, but watch out for my little sister. She's lurking inside somewhere." Then she rushed out the door clutching a slide case and her purse.

"Want to use my car?" he yelled, but she was already climbing into the pickup truck that had "Murphy's Tree

Farm" stenciled on its side. The truck growled into action. It didn't surprise Jamie that Louisa could drive a truck. He believed she could do everything.

Alone, he looked curiously around the big kitchen for clues to her life. Kids' drawings covered the only wall that had no cabinets. Eight mismatched chairs surrounded a long wooden table. Eight for dinner? Jamie imagined nightly parties. If only he'd been lucky enough to be born into a big family!

He ambled through a passageway lined with shelves of food on one side, and on the other, shelves of well-used board games with sprung cardboard sides. It would be a family that played together, of course. The dining room had a cot, thinly disguised with pillows, along one wall. A dress pattern pinned to material lay on the dining room table, and the sideboard was full of wildly growing vines reaching for the top of the many-paned window.

The living room was dim because of the snow-laden day outside, but in the corner was a brightly lit Christmas tree strung with cranberry and popcorn garlands. Jamie liked the homemade tree decorations and the worn, comfortable furnishings of the rest of the room. A stuffed dog next to a sewing basket and a slither of magazines took up half the couch. A football sprouted from the center of the fruit bowl on the cocktail table like a strange brown cactus. One lamp sported six blown-up balloons attached by string. A child's lunch box rested on the arm of an upholstered chair with an enticingly soft lap.

Jamie started toward the chair, but was transfixed by a voice from behind the swagged draperies that framed the big bay window.

"Are you a robber?" the voice demanded.

"No, I'm Louisa's friend Jamie," he replied. "Who are you?"

"May."

"May you what?"

"May's my name, and I hate name jokes." A twiggy girl child with a ferocious expression emerged from the drape to scowl at him. "They're stupid and rotten and mean."

"I wasn't joking," Jamie said mildly, "just being dense. You, I take it, are never dense?"

"Never."

"Well, you're lucky." He removed the lunch box and perched on the arm of the chair, ready for further conversational sparring.

"What did you come here for?" May now asked.

"Your sister invited me. It's official. Want to shake hands and say hello?" He held out his hand. She approached with great dignity and shook it.

"Would you like to hear what I wrote about you?" May asked.

Jamie guessed this gypsy waif was about ten, as unlike her sister as she could look. "I thought you didn't know who I was."

"I didn't. These are observations from when you didn't know I was in the room. I'm developing visual acuity."

"You're developing what?"

"Acuity," she repeated, frowning at him as if he were indeed dense. "I'm going to be a reporter."

She flipped open the notepad in her hand and read aloud. "Strange footsteps. He's casing our living room. Too nice looking to be a burglar. Too short to be one of Lou's boyfriends."

29

"I'm five ten. That's not short," Jamie objected.

"You're not five ten," May said loftily. "That's how tall Louisa is, and you don't look anywhere as big as her."

"Well, I am. If I look shorter, it's probably because she wears heels."

"Louisa'd never wear heels," May said. "She wears the flattest shoes she can find, and she won't wear full skirts or plaid either."

"Why?"

"Because she hates being big. Personally, I think she's read too many yucky love stories where dainty little females swoon in some godzilla's arms."

Jamie laughed.

"It's not funny," May said. "She'll diet herself to death some day. She was even considering saving up for that operation where they cut pieces out of your leg bones to make you shorter. Ugh!"

"Crazy," Jamie said. "She's beautiful just as she is."

"That's what my father tells her, but she says he's only trying to make her feel better because she came out looking like him. I wish I looked like my father instead of my mother. My mother's a peanut."

"Hey," he said. "Being small is an advantage to a reporter. You can watch people without them noticing you."

"I never thought of that." She looked at him with new respect. Then she squinted and added slyly, "You like Louisa a lot, don't you?"

"Everybody likes her."

"Not everybody," May corrected. "She's too bossy, and she makes my brothers and me mad lots of times. Only I love her anyway because she's the only person in this family who talks to me—except sometimes my father, but he forgets to listen. And my *brothers!*" Her eyes rolled for emphasis. "All they know how to do is tease."

Jamie laughed. "Sounds like a tough life."

"You don't think so?" May sounded offended.

"I wouldn't know." He tried to tone down his smile.

"Anyway, the only one Louisa isn't bossy with is Vincent. Her boyfriend? Around him, she acts like she doesn't know her own mind. She does everything he says."

"Everything?" Jamie asked anxiously.

"Everything that isn't against her principles. She has lots of principles. *I* don't. I think principles get in a person's way."

"They do that," Jamie agreed, rolling his lower lip out and nodding wisely. "And what principles does Louisa go by?"

"Oh, you know," May said with an airy wave of her hand. "She thinks you should be honest with everyone, and improve the world you live in and be on time and keep your room clean and not drink too much or smoke or have sex before marriage. At least, that's what she *says,* but the way she acts with Vince, I'm not so sure she means it about the sex."

Jamie's groan was lost in Louisa's shout: "May Alexandra Murphy!"

There were several seconds of silence during which May shrank to mouselike proportions.

"How dare you talk that way about me to my friends? What kind of ratfink exposes her own sister's secrets?"

"I wasn't telling him any secrets, just my opinions," May said, holding her small chin up.

"Shameless, that's what you are. You're going to wind up as a reporter for some terrible scandal sheet that prints nothing but lies."

Jamie couldn't gauge Louisa's anger, but May suddenly flew across the room and grasped her sister as if Louisa were a tree trunk. "I'm sorry," May squealed. "Don't yell at me, Louisa. I hate it when you're mad at me."

Louisa's voice softened. "Then don't go talking about me behind my back."

"I won't. You can trust me."

"Can I?" Louisa disentangled herself from May's embrace. "Then I suppose you've cleaned up the guinea pig's mess in your room like you promised this morning?"

"I would have," May said. "But I've been entertaining your friend." Jamie blinked at the supersonic speed with which May had recovered her cool.

Louisa sucked in her cheeks and squinted at her sister. Then she told May, "You get that room cleaned up right now, you little conniver, or that guinea pig moves to the basement."

May stood up straight and said, "You know Glorious would die if you made her live in the basement, and anyway, you're getting bossy again." She took a wary step backward. "Now don't get mad at me. Remember, you told me to tell you when."

"I wouldn't have to boss you around if you did what you're supposed to do," Louisa said. "March!" She pointed to the stairs and May raced for them. They heard the pattering of her feet going up, but when Jamie turned to share a smile with Louisa, he was amazed to see tears glossing her eyes.

"What's the matter?" he asked.

"I can't stand it," Louisa said. "No matter how hard I try not to be, I act bossy. I just can't seem to stop myself from running things."

"What's wrong with your running things?" Jamie asked. "You do it better than anyone else."

"Jamie, you don't need to be nice. Even you called me bossy. Remember, Christmas Eve when you bought your tree?"

"That's because you made me angry."

"Right. I make a lot of people angry. Nobody likes to be pushed around and told what to do all the time. In fourth grade, I was hurt because everybody hated me, and I couldn't see why. I tried to change when I finally understood what was wrong, and I keep hoping I have, but I haven't."

"You're crazy. How'd you get to be class president in seventh grade if nobody appreciated you?"

"Well . . . but I was more diplomatic by seventh grade. I'm okay if I think before I open my mouth, but it's hard for me. You can't believe how frustrating it is to try and change your basic personality."

"Yes, I can," he said. "Remember me, Louisa? The kid with all the bad habits?"

She exhaled and smiled at him mistily. "You and I have a lot in common, don't we?"

"More than you think." He reached out to take her in his arms, but she shook her head and evaded him, curling up in the soft-lapped chair with her legs tucked under her.

He had a sudden urge to confide that it was he who had sent her the unsigned valentine she'd gotten in eighth grade,

33

but she had started talking about her father. She'd remember that valentine; it had been the fanciest one in the card shop. He hadn't signed it because he was afraid she'd laugh at him. One good thing about maturing was he no longer minded being laughed at.

". . . and Pops hadn't even missed his slides. He was still busy entertaining his bird watchers with stories when I arrived. Did you ever have my father for social studies, Jamie?"

"No, but I've heard he's a good teacher."

"A great teacher," Louisa corrected. "Kids like him because he's easy and jokes a lot, but besides that he knows more history than anybody. In fact, the only things Pops really does remember are what happened hundreds of years ago."

"You like him, huh?"

"I like everybody in our family, especially the little character you just met. That child! She cracks me up with all her airs."

"She's cute," Jamie agreed.

"She and her guinea pig! May's mad about Glorious. In her list of favorites, May puts Glorious second, right after me and Pops. Mother is third, and Jeff and Billy come near the bottom because they tease her so much. Speaking of which—they haven't shown up yet, have they?"

"Your brothers? They probably found some really good tracks to follow. How come your mother comes in the middle of May's list? Doesn't she like guinea pigs?"

"Oh, Mother's got nothing against guinea pigs. . . ." Louisa considered. "Mother is the practical one in this family—the one who does everything? She's the one who taught me how to sew and cook and do carpentry, but May doesn't like to do physical things."

"Carpentry?" Jamie asked.

"Mother was a carpenter when Pops met her. He says he noticed her because she was the smallest carpenter he'd ever seen. At first, he didn't realize she was a woman."

Jamie grinned. He envisioned an older version of May balancing a floor joist on her shoulder. "Does she still hammer any nails?"

"She does *all* the repairs around this place. Dad's the philosopher and Mother is the little dynamo doer."

"Like her daughter."

"Oh, I have her energy, but otherwise we're very different. She doesn't have this compulsion to organize people that I suffer from. All Mother wants is to be left alone so she can devote herself to being a real estate person, which is fine, except I worry that the kids aren't getting the discipline they need, and that's why I end up—oh well, enough about me. Did your father like the Christmas tree?"

"Sort of." Jamie shrugged off her question. When he'd returned from working at the tennis club last night, Jake had been reading a medical journal in the living room. He'd looked up and said gruffly, "You did a good job." Jamie had been pleased until he realized the compliment more likely referred to the clean-up job he'd done on the mess in the living room than to his decorating efforts.

"So what did you get for Christmas?" Louisa asked next with an impish grin. "Remember when we were little kids and couldn't wait to get to school and tell everybody what we got for Christmas?"

"All I got was money," Jamie said. "How about you?"

She laughed. "Mostly clothes that don't fit except for a stuffed bird May made for me. That was my best gift."

35

Jamie socked his forehead with the heel of his hand. "I should have bought you a Christmas present."

"Why? We've never exchanged presents before."

"No," he said, "but . . . ." She'd never invited him into her life before. She had now and he was hoping it wasn't for just this one time. "So what're your plans for this week?" he asked.

"I'll do some sewing and some ice-skating with the kids. See Vince. Just fool around, you know. How about you?"

"Not much," he said. "Probably get at some of those college applications I have to do. That's a job I really hate."

"You haven't done your college applications yet? Jamie, that's awful. You should always do the things you hate most first. That way you get the worst over with and can relax and enjoy the time that's left." She groaned. "Listen to me. I'm at it again."

"Hey," he said. "I could use someone to manage my life. Want the job?"

"You're too nice to me," she said. "Come on out to the kitchen and help me get lunch on the table. You'll stay, won't you?"

He was glad to stay. Her brothers arrived as she was heating up a pot of homemade vegetable soup. They claimed they'd seen bear tracks on the hill, and when Louisa showed her doubt, they all had to trek out to where the alleged bear tracks were impressed in the remains of the light snow that had fallen during the night. Louisa suggested a large dog and some natural melting around the paw prints as most likely, but Jamie won points with the boys by saying, "It could be a bear. Why not? Stranger things have happened."

36

After lunch, May took Jamie up to her room, now clean and sprayed with floral-scented deodorant, and Jamie agreed solemnly that the golden mop with the gopher face was truly a well-named guinea pig. As he was picking his way over the ingeniously built maze of scrap lumber, tin cans, and wire mesh which was Glorious's run and which covered all available floor space in May's room, she said, "You're a lot cuter than Vince, and nicer, too. If Louisa doesn't ask you, you can always come to see me."

"I like you, too, kid," Jamie said.

Louisa's father wandered in and give Jamie an impromptu lecture on the possibility of Indian settlements on the site where Jamie's condominium was built. Jamie listened, fascinated, but he jumped up to leave when Louisa said she had to get ready for Vince, who was picking her up to take her to a party. "Stop by again," Louisa told him warmly. "It's so nice to have a chance to really talk to you, Jamie."

"Don't worry, I'll be back," he said, and was grateful enough to add, "You have a good time with Vince tonight."

He drove home thinking about how much he liked all the Murphys he'd met so far and how incredible it was that Louisa shouldn't know what a wonderful, beautiful girl she was. Crazy for her to want to repress her leadership talent. That was probably why he hadn't noticed her name in the political arena in school for so long. She was class secretary only because she'd been asked to fill in when the boy who'd been elected had to move away, and her other activities weren't very newsworthy. It would be a shame if she wasted her ability. What he should do was try to convince her that her bossiness had its uses. He could offer himself as her campaign manager whenever she decided to run for President.

His noble intentions caused him to censor the sexy parts of his daydreams about Louisa as he lay in his bed that night. He'd go back to visit her soon. It was possible that she'd start seeing him in a more romantic light. After all, the size of a guy's heart had to matter more in the long run than how big he was physically. Yes, he'd go back soon. Vincent Brunelli couldn't be as unbeatable as he looked.

4

ONE AFTERNOON in January, the coach asked Jamie if he wanted to go out for the vaulting in the gymnastics meet coming up with Shaker High. "Do I have a chance to win?"

"I wouldn't ask you if you didn't," the coach said.

Jamie was surprised, then pleased, then excited. He agreed to double his usual practice time and rushed off to tell Louisa. She was involved in so many afterschool activities that she usually took the late bus home, and he'd taken to hanging around himself so he could either ride with her or offer her a lift in his car.

Sure enough, Louisa was in a meeting, heading it as usual. The handwritten sign on the door said, "Volunteer tutors meet here."

"Most of these little kids aren't dumb," Louisa was telling a dozen, mostly female candidates. "They just need some one-to-one attention in reading or math. Lots of them have nobody at home who has time for them. Just giving them some of your time would help."

He listened, leaning against the doorjamb, half-persuaded he should volunteer, too. Maybe after the gymnastics meet he'd do it. A teacher got up to talk to the group, and Jamie caught Louisa's eye and beckoned her out into the hall. "Do something for me?" he asked.

"What, Jamie? I'm busy."

"Promise to come to the gym two weeks from Thursday night at eight."

"Why?"

He wanted to stroke away the creases her frown made; he wanted to kiss her, but he didn't dare do either. Instead he said, "Just promise. Come on. I need you there."

"Are you going to be in the gymnastics meet?"

"You got it."

"Then sure, I'll try to come."

"You're so beautiful," he murmured and kissed her nose. She shoved him lightly, and he pretended to stagger backward across the hall, but she ducked back into the classroom unimpressed. He walked off resolving to begin intensive daily practice. He would learn to fly over that horse like Spiderman, Superman, a circus acrobat at least. He would make Louisa fall in love with him by the veritable grace of his fantastic twenty-second leap over that cylindrical brown leather monster. Sure he would.

*   *   *   *

The extra hours Jamie spent after school in the gym meant he had less time to drop by Louisa's house, which had been his habit since Christmas. Evenings, when he showed up, she was often busy with Vince or just out somewhere.

After the first week of his arduous practice schedule, May greeted Jamie at the kitchen door one night, hands on her narrow hips. "Where were you this afternoon when I needed you? Mother had a hot real estate prospect, and there wasn't anybody here to drive me to chorus."

"I'm sorry, May. I'm practicing to be a star gymnast."

"That's okay, but what about me? They need me in chorus, you know."

He apologized, amused to find that chauffeuring her twice to appointments obligated him for steady duty in her eyes.

"Why do you want to be a star gymnast?" May asked. "Isn't that just for girls?"

"No way. It's an equal opportunity sport. The coach says I just might win the vaulting competition in the next meet, and your sister's coming to watch me."

"Can I come, too?"

"Sure, if she'll bring you."

"I know what you want," May said sagely. "You want to impress Louisa by winning."

"You got it. Think I have a chance?"

"No. Bozo's got her all tied up. They spent a whole hour last night down here kissing when they were supposed to be baby-sitting."

Jamie's heart sagged at the image of his girl in Vince's arms. "How come you call him Bozo?" he ignored his pain to ask.

"Because he does this clown act with me, trying to make me like him, but he doesn't like me or my brothers much."

"How can you tell?"

"I know when someone thinks I'm a pest."

"Vince is one impressive guy, May," Jamie said. "He's big and smart and— They already accepted him at MIT, I think." Jamie pushed away the thought of his own incomplete college application forms. He hadn't been able to force himself to it yet, although he had spent hours trying.

"Vince isn't so smart. He never says anything, just sits around grabbing at Louisa and eating up all the potato chips," May said.

It comforted Jamie to have May on his side, despite the twinge her lowdown on Louisa's love life gave him. Bozo, whatever May thought of him, was a challenging rival. Maybe a flying leap over a leather horse wouldn't do enough, but offhand, Jamie couldn't think of anything better.

Jeff and Billy came rampaging through the kitchen, nearly knocking May over in their haste. "Hey, Jamie, wanta help us make a toboggan run tomorrow?" Jeff asked, man to man.

"There isn't enough snow for a toboggan run," Jamie said.

"Yeah, but we're supposed to get a foot tonight."

"Okay, if we do, I'll help. You pass that math test we studied for last week?"

"Yeah, I did," Jeff blushed deeply.

"He cheated," Billy said.

"Only one answer, just one. Don't tell Louisa, Jamie. She'll kill me," Jeff begged.

"You promise not to cheat anymore and I won't tell," Jamie said, imitating Louisa's manner. "Cheating's as bad for your health as smoking or drinking."

Jeff nodded and he and Billy scuttled out of the room before Jamie could develop his lecture any further.

"You sound just like Louisa," May said. "She's a prude, too."

"She's not a prude," Jamie said, "or she wouldn't have sat around kissing Bozo last night."

"Oh, kissing!" May said, as if in her vast experience, kissing was nothing.

"You are going to be one tough lady when you grow up," Jamie told her.

Just then Mrs. Murphy popped into the room. She was a wren-sized woman with a brisk, no-nonsense air about her who treated Jamie as if he were only another of her numerous children underfoot.

Today, without greeting him, she demanded, "Where's Louisa, Jamie? May? Did she get everybody fed? I have to grab a sandwich myself and get over to the Bowder farm. They're finally getting ready to sell, and I have a hot prospect in my back pocket if we can just move fast enough."

"Louisa's upstairs," May said. "She has a headache. I think she had a fight with Vincent."

"Did she?" Jamie asked hopefully.

"Oh, it'll blow over," Mrs. Murphy said. "Those two are always arguing. May! Did you cut up my latest *House Beautiful?* I haven't even seen this issue yet." She glared at her youngest daughter.

"Don't look at me," May said.

"Then where are your brothers?"

"They went thataway." May pointed and her mother charged off. They heard her tapping up the stairs to chew out her sons.

"I hope she doesn't yell at them too hard," May said. "Jamie, I can't talk to you anymore. I have to hide."

43

"From what?"

"From when she finds out I was the one who cut up her magazine."

"You sicked her on your brothers when they're innocent?" Jamie asked.

"So what? It won't bother them because they didn't do it, but I can't stand getting yelled at. That's why I cut up the stupid magazine in the first place. I wrote a ten-page story for my English teacher and she wouldn't accept it because it wasn't illustrated. The assignment was an illustrated book and I can't draw at all. I just cut out a few pictures of houses and families. See you." She flipped around the corner of the kitchen and took off into regions of the house where Jamie had never been.

Jamie was just letting himself out the back door when Louisa called his name. "I didn't know you were here," she said.

"May was entertaining me. So were your brothers and mother. Your family's very entertaining. How's your headache?"

"Gone." She yawned. "I'm going to make some cocoa. Want some?"

"Sure." He set out cups while she mixed the milk and cocoa in a pot on the stove.

"You must really be practicing for that meet, Jamie. I've hardly seen you this past week," Louisa said.

"You missed me?" he asked. "Great God in heaven, she missed me!" He got down on his knees and clasped his hands in gratitude.

"Calm down," she said. "It was May who noticed you

haven't been by much. I've been too busy. Not that I don't like having you around but—"

"You're still coming to the meet, aren't you?"

"If I can."

"You promised."

"Jamie, sometimes you sound about as old as my little brothers."

"All right. I'll be mature." He deepened his voice. "You promised."

She laughed. "I did, and I'll be there." She poured the cocoa into the cups and sent him to find paper napkins in the pantry.

"How's it going with your father?" she asked when he sat down.

"He's still hung up on my neglected college applications."

"You could fix that easy enough."

"It's not easy. Those essays! What am I going to write about my goals and philosophy of life? It sounds dumb to say I want to grow up to be a doctor like my father."

"No, it doesn't sound dumb. You could say that."

"It's one sentence. They want five hundred words or more."

"You're just making up excuses."

"Maybe I'll go to a community college for the first couple of years."

"Why should you when you can afford to go anywhere? Your marks aren't that bad, and I'll bet you did well on the SAT's."

"Listen," he said. "You're the one who could get in anywhere you wanted. They'd give you a scholarship easy with your grades and all the extracurricular stuff you do."

"I'm not doing much this year."

"Oh, come on! Secretary of the senior class. Christmas fund director again, the volunteer tutors, volleyball—and senior year hardly counts anyway."

She smiled. "Now who's keeping track of whom?"

"Well, you're not the only one who cares about old classmates," he said.

"Okay, but until I make up my mind what I want out of life, I might just as well go to a state college near home and save money," she stated flatly.

"*You* don't know what you want to do? I can't believe that," Jamie said. "How about going for law? I could see you as a judge. Or how about Senator Louisa Murphy? You could wind up as our first woman President."

"Forget it," she said. "I've outgrown that phase."

"What phase?"

"You know, where I thought I knew best. Where I wanted to run the world. I'm not that bossy kid I used to be."

"What a loss!"

"You don't understand, Jamie. Believe me, it's no fun being the leader. You know what happens to you? You're all alone up there working hard while everybody else is fooling around and either resenting you or criticizing the way you're doing things. Sure, I like getting things done, but I want time to spend with my family and friends. I'm tired of running from one meeting to the next with my head full of details that have to be accomplished yesterday. Can you see what I'm saying?" She leaned forward, intent on his reaction.

He shrugged and admitted, "I always figured on boasting I knew you when. You're not going to settle for being Vince Brunelli's housewife and nothing else, are you?"

"Why not? I'll still be me. Maybe my career will be marriage and raising ten children. I don't have to run for President to prove myself."

"No, you don't. It's just that a talent that doesn't get used . . . ." He hesitated, not wanting to lecture. "I just thought you'd make a great President someday, that's all."

She relented. "Well, don't give up on me altogether. I've still got this ambition to run things, and who knows how long I can control it? Sometimes it makes me crazy. I go around wrestling with myself as if I'm two persons in one skin."

"I know that feeling."

"Do you?" She looked at him thoughtfully. "I suppose you might. . . . See, I had two grandmothers who were both exceptionally strong ladies. One was a school principal and the other ran a garage. I never met either of them, but I don't want to be accused of being the kind of domineering woman their children claimed they were. Their kids all left home early and their husbands either died or deserted them. I want to be strong, yes, but in a soft, feminine way."

"So don't be a cactus," he said, "but wouldn't you rather be a tree than a flower?" He hurried past her questioning frown. "I mean, feminine . . . what does feminine mean?"

"I'd love to be a flower," she said.

"Why? They don't last, but trees do."

"Flowers are what you give people on special occasions and they smell good and they're beautiful."

"So are trees, which also give shade and provide wood, and face it, Louisa, you're a tree. You're basically a tree."

"Because you say so?" She sounded indignant. "Why do I have to be what you want me to be?"

"You don't, but maybe you shouldn't struggle so hard against your own nature. Does Vince go for flowers?"

47

"Your metaphor is silly, Jamie, but yes, he does."

"Then maybe you need to find yourself a tree lover. Try me, for instance. I'm easy to get along with and a whiz at computer games."

"I love you, Jamie," she said gently. "I really do—like a brother."

"Done for!" he groaned and struck his forehead with the heel of his hand.

"Where's May?" Mrs. Murphy whipped into the kitchen. "*She's* the one who did in my magazine."

"If she is, you'll never find her, Ma," Louisa said. "How did you make out with the people from Wichita?"

"Possible. They're sort of interested. But tonight I've got to see about that farm property with the view I told you about. If I can pull that deal off, you can go to Alfred and do ceramics after all, Louisa. Wish us both luck." She hugged her daughter and sped off.

"Alfred, huh?" Jamie said. "You never told me you wanted to do ceramics."

"I haven't decided on it definitely. It interests me—the idea of working with my hands and creating beautiful, useful things. But my parents don't have any money. Putting my older brothers through school left them in debt, and now, besides me, there's May and the boys to worry about, and it's all on Mother's shoulders. Dad's darling, but he's allergic to anything to do with money, so she has to handle it. Even the tree farm is basically her business. It's best if I stay around while they need my help."

He watched the play of emotions on her face. Even if she never loved him back, he couldn't help but adore her. She was so rich in depths and color. A guy as self-involved as

48

Vince would never properly appreciate her. It wasn't fair. She was wasting her feelings on the wrong man.

"Jamie," Louisa said. "Would you tell me something I've always wondered about?"

"Anything you want to know," he said.

"What was your mother like?"

She'd never asked him about his mother, never said anything to him when she found out his mother had died except that she was sorry. He looked into her sympathetic blue eyes, at the fine skin taut over the strong bones of her face, and he was glad that she cared enough about him to ask that question.

"My mother was pretty and lively. She liked to have fun," he said, his speech plodding because he hadn't talked about his mother in so long.

"And?"

"And she loved me a lot. She was always on my side. But she was moody, and she liked to do crazy things."

"Like what?"

"Well, there were nice things like parties for squirrels and sad things like pretending she was dead."

"Huh?"

He shrugged, suddenly too weary to explain, but Louisa was waiting patiently, so he continued. "Well, once when I was about eight, I tried to wake her up from a nap and she acted dead. So I got hysterical and called my father. They'd just taught me to dial the number that was written on the wall next to the telephone. He came home and shut the bedroom door and later I heard her laughing. She wasn't dead, just wanted to see if he'd come if she needed him."

"That was cruel."

49

Jamie remembered how his heart had hammered halfway through the walls of his chest. He'd never been more scared than he was that afternoon. "She didn't mean to be," he said.

"Did you love her more than your father?"

"Oh, yeah. She was the biggest thing in my life. I was a terrible Mama's boy."

"Poor Jamie," Louisa said. "But maybe you're better off growing up without her?"

"Maybe," he said, though he didn't believe it.

Louisa's father got in from a meeting at school and announced that the roads were getting bad. Two inches of snow had already fallen and it was coming down hard. "How're the tires on that old car of yours, Jamie?" he asked. His handsome, leonine face had only the glasses and the edge of gray around his receding hairline to show his age. His smile was as wide and warm as Louisa's. "You might want to bunk on our couch for the night. Better than sliding into a ditch."

"I've got snow tires, but thanks, Mr. Murphy," Jamie said. They were all so nice to him. Just as nice as they were to Vince, probably, just as nice as they'd be to anybody. It was their nature to be nice.

Jamie drove home carefully into the snowflakes that came at him like a million blips on the space game screen, only to be wiped out by the blade of his windshield wiper while he concentrated on staying parallel to the white posts that ran along the outside edge of the road. "Progress report on your infiltration of the young woman's affections?" he asked himself and answered, "Progress so far, zilch."

50

◄5►

BEING IN LOVE with someone who was in love with someone else was painful. Jamie would witness the joyful anticipation with which Louisa got ready for a date with Vince and wonder at his own masochism that he continued to play the part of friend when it hurt so much to be reminded that that was all he was. Often the most satisfying part of Jamie's day began late at night when he had left the other-world abstraction of the game room and returned to the darkened apartment where the silence was broken only by the cluck of the heating ducts and the hum of the refrigerator. He would pass his father's bedroom and listen for the snore that meant Jake was sloughing off the weariness of another day. A quick shower, then Jamie would ease into his cold bed and begin the elaborate scenarios in which Louisa finally succumbed to his passion for her.

Sometimes he won her with deeds of self-sacrifice or daring. After he offered her his kidney or carried her from a burning building, she would turn to him and confess that she had changed her mind. It was Jamie whom she loved best after all.

In his dreams he would finally hold her in his arms and revel in tingling love-making. She was his, as magnetized by him as he was by her. "Louisa," he would moan in the hollow of his bed, "Louisa, I love you."

*   *   *   *

"You're looking peaked. You ought to get more exercise," his father said toward the end of January when Jamie had been practicing several hours after school each day in preparation for the meet with Shaker High.

"I'm exercising plenty, Dad. I'm going to be in a gymnastics competition next week. Want to come watch me?"

"Men's gymnastics? That's not much of a spectator sport, is it? More like glorified exercises."

"Yeah," Jamie said. "You could look at it that way."

"If you'd been willing to work at it, you would have made a decent tennis player."

"Except I happen to like gymnastics. Your sports are racquet ball and golf, mine is gymnastics. Okay, Dad?"

"I don't *like* racquet ball and golf particularly. They keep me in shape, that's all. Physical activity relieves tension."

"I know," Jamie said.

Jake shrugged and switched subjects. "Hear from any colleges yet?"

They were sharing a steak and frozen baked stuffed potatoes and salad for dinner, standard fare except Jamie had used artichokes in the salad for a change. If Jake noticed any dif-

52

ference, he didn't comment on it. Scratch artichokes, Jamie thought. No sense getting fancy when Jake didn't care what he ate so long as it had onions in it.

"You don't hear from schools until April," Jamie stalled.

"Some of them report sooner, I understand," Jake said. He wolfed the rest of his steak and poured them each a cup of coffee. The coffee-making was his department.

If he didn't get in, he could put a gun to his head or go join the Foreign Legion, Jamie thought. Or he could leave home and just bum around the country. Maybe try the far West and see if he could get a job in the oilfields.

"You're not . . . doing anything stupid again, are you?" his father asked with more subtlety than usual.

"Don't worry. I'm clean," Jamie said.

He'd been thirteen the morning his father had grabbed him by the shoulders, peered into his eyes and announced, "You're doing drugs. What are you taking?"

"Nothing," Jamie had lied. He'd been so scared of his father at thirteen that Jake could make him jump just by giving him a hard look or a short criticism. Jamie had considered himself lucky that most of the time his father barely noticed him. They'd moved from the big house to the more efficient condominium without Jake's even once asking Jamie how he felt about it. Jake consulted him no more than he would an inanimate object or a household pet. Then all of a sudden that morning, Jake began paying attention to his son.

"What are you taking?" Jake had demanded again.

"Not much," Jamie had said, terrified by Jake's tightened lips.

Silence and more grim-faced staring on Jake's part.

53

"I've got to get to school," Jamie had tried.

"No, you don't. Not today. I'm not letting you out of my sight until we work this out."

Jake had kept him on a short leash, figuratively, with the admonition to "stay with me." All day, Jamie had followed his father through Jake's rounds, everywhere but into the operating room. Then his father had told a nurse with plum-ripe lips, "Put him to work, Miss Lyons. Keep him busy, will you?"

Miss Lyons had smiled and told Jamie, "I'm going to work your tail off, little Landes." She had, too. She'd made him fetch and carry vases for flowers, pitchers of water, chairs for visitors, even bedpans, until he was tired.

On the way home from the hospital, while they were eating dinner at a diner, Jake had said, "I took a week off. Your school's been informed. We're going to hike the Appalachian Trail together, or some of it. Okay?"

Jamie hadn't known whether to be glad or not. He didn't like being around Jake. He didn't feel all that well without the pot to get him through the day, and he was tired before they'd even started. But the Appalachian Trail was an adventure he'd read about. Other kids he knew did things with their fathers. Maybe he wouldn't be so scared of Jake if they went hiking together. By the time Jamie had his backpack loaded and the new cook kit and camp stove were bought and ready, he was looking forward to the trip.

That bright April midweek morning, they'd driven off with sleeping bags and backpacks and stopped at the mountaineering store to buy the dried food and trail guides they needed. It hadn't been a perfect week, but not once had his father lectured him on drugs. Jamie had been miserable with aches and exhausted trying to keep up with Jake, but he'd appreciated that his father wasn't lecturing him. It rained and they got wet and they'd lost some of their gear to marauding raccoons. Jake hadn't said much until the last night, and then it was only two sentences: "You're all I've got, son. If you do yourself in, you're doing me in, too." Jamie had gone cold hearing his father say that, and he'd suddenly believed what his mother had told him when she left. His father did need him, after all.

Jamie didn't care much about what he did with his own life, but he couldn't imagine being careless with his father's. So he'd avoided the boys' bathroom nearest his homeroom for the rest of eighth grade, and he'd kept away from the edge of the parking lot where the woods began and steered clear of the guys who sold pot and sometimes unlabeled pills from their lockers.

He'd gone off to high school feeling confident that he'd never be one of the zonked-out kids who sleepwalked through the school day and got suspended for cutting classes and sometimes wound up in the hospital for drug-related accidents or in the newspaper for drug-related crimes. He felt for those kids, but they were different from him. He had a purpose. He would grow up to be a doctor like his dad and be a credit to him. He'd told Jake this new ambition to please him, but Jake had merely nodded and said, "I hope so, Jamie."

The new friends in high school were fun guys, always kidding around. They didn't do drugs, but they drank a fair amount. And in high school he'd found Ginny, who was small and soft and liked to cuddle. She'd satisfied Jamie's hunger for affection, and, finally, for sex. He knew he was lucky they hadn't ended up having to get married. He hadn't been in love with her, and they were both too young anyway, but he missed all that touching and sweet talk.

Despite the occasional effort Jake made to connect with Jamie on vacations, Jamie still didn't feel he knew his father. For one thing, Jake had never said a word about his feelings when his wife left him. Either he couldn't or he wouldn't talk about it. He never criticized her, either, and Jamie admired that. He didn't think it was fair of his mother to voice all her complaints about Jake to Jamie. Jake's silence was nicer.

The only time Jake showed he felt something for the wife he'd lost was two years ago when they got word that she'd died. That night, Jamie had been awakened by raucous sounds, frightening sounds. He had tiptoed to the door of his father's bedroom and peeked in. Jake was lying face down in his pillow on his bed, making noises that sounded like an agonized wrenching of cavernous machinery, as if the depths of his soul were being ground up. It was so awesome that Jamie had made no attempt to comfort his father. He'd crept back the way he'd come and hidden from that awful grief under his own pillow.

Jamie found his own reactions odd, too. He hadn't quite believed his mother was dead, not for months, and then he'd suffered short spasms of anger that came and went at unexpected moments. He'd relieved his pain with frequent infusions of alcohol. He hadn't drunk as much as his buddies before his mother died, but afterward, he drank a whole lot

56

more. Alcohol didn't strike him as truly dangerous, no matter what he read or heard about it. At least, that was his conviction until the night he nearly killed himself on the way home from an all-male beer bash.

This time, there hadn't been a camping trip. Instead, contempt laced his father's voice when he said, "If it isn't one poison, it's another. What's your problem, Jamie? You're getting too old to need so much parental attention."

"Sorry, Dad. I guess I should have known better. But there's nothing wrong, really."

"Nothing wrong? First drugs, now alcohol. What are you running from?"

"I don't know. I didn't think. I mean, I didn't think I was drinking too much."

"You seem to have a propensity for excess, and that's bad news for your future unless you can get control of yourself."

The upshot was that Jamie had spent most of his free time that summer seeing a shrink, actually a psychologist, a woman who seemed to understand him better than he'd ever understood himself.

"Why do you think your mother ran away?" she'd asked him, after he had begun to trust her enough to stop answering "I don't know" to all her questions.

"Because she wasn't satisfied with her life with us."

"With you and your father?"

"Yeah."

"What did you have to do with her dissatisfaction?" Dr. Britain had asked, her clear eyes holding him to an honest answer.

"Not much. It was mostly my father she complained about,

how he never came home and didn't want to do anything fun. She called him 'Old Stone Face.' She called him worse things, too."

"But she was satisfied with you?"

"Sure. She loved me a lot when I was little. She was always my side." Once his mother had even said she would have died of unhappiness if she hadn't had Jamie, but he didn't boast to Dr. Britain about that well-remembered line. Instead, he said, "I guess I wasn't enough for her, though. After she left—"

"Yes?"

"After she left, I felt like I'd failed her. Dumb things—like maybe I shouldn't have spent time playing with other kids and should've stayed home and kept her company. If I'd been funnier and could have made her laugh more—"

"Do you still feel guilty?"

"No. I know it wasn't me."

"But she left you. Does that make you angry?"

"No. She had to think about her own life, but— Sometimes I'd get mad, and I'd think she should have taken me along. I'd have been a lot better off with her in Jamaica even if the schools were bad like she claimed. I used to wish I was black so she'd love me. . . . Dumb things like that. You know."

"Do you still miss her?"

"Not anymore. Anyway, she's dead now. . . . My father and I get along okay without her. It's just—"

"Just what?"

"That I miss her, and I'll never see her again." The moisture in his eyes betrayed him and he turned his head away angrily.

"It's all right, Jamie," Dr. Britain said. "It's good to grieve. It's all right to feel sad."

"I'm too old to miss my mother."

"Nobody's too old to miss someone they love."

He considered the absolute ring of truth to that and asked, "You know what I missed most? Getting hugged and kissed. That's what I still miss most. I guess I'm emotionally retarded."

"Isn't your father affectionate?"

"No."

"Ever try hugging or kissing him?"

Jamie laughed. "You don't know my father."

"But he's sad, too, because he misses her. You and he have that in common. You should talk to him about it, about how he feels and how you feel."

"I can't," Jamie had declared. "I don't know how."

When they talked about his drinking, she wouldn't accept that he drank to forget. "There's more to it than that," Dr. Britain had said. "You just don't have a high enough regard for yourself. You don't appreciate your own good qualities."

When he had pushed her for what they were, she'd made him name them. Yes, he was an honest, upright, sympathetic person who liked other people and felt for them when he wasn't in too much pain for himself to feel for anybody else. Yes, he got along easily with the rest of the human race. Yes, he was intelligent enough to do pretty much whatever he wanted, although he wasn't as brilliant as he'd like to be or especially talented at anything. And he was agile and well coordinated. And he was good looking. So he was okay, basically, just lonely for the moment and overwhelmed by his father.

59

"Lots of healthy extracurricular activities," she'd advised. "Go out for sports and be sure you eat three good meals a day. Get enough sleep." And she'd added, "Get yourself a nice girlfriend to have fun with."

"What kind of fun, Dr. Britain?" he'd teased.

"Love is the healthiest outlet you can find," she'd answered, without giving an inch.

He'd liked that clear-eyed lady. Too bad she'd convinced him that he was well enough to do without her anymore.

‹6›

Jamie felt as if he were running double time in the days just before the meet with Shaker. He had neglected his schoolwork to get in the daily stint of practice in the gym and spend most evenings sitting around Louisa's house keeping an eye on her. Now his English teacher warned that if Jamie didn't immediately produce the three vocabulary exercises and two essays long past due, he'd fail the third quarter which ended on Thursday, the day of the meet.

Luckily, school was closed for a district teacher's conference, so he had that day to catch up. He got up early and had hacked his way through the vocabulary work, which was drudgery enough to give him a headache, when the phone rang.

A girlish voice asked timidly, "Jamie?"

"Yah, who's this?"

The voice gained confidence. "It's May. You better get over here fast."

"What happened?"

"Mom went with Dad for a school visitation in Vermont, so they're gone for the day, and Bozo's here acting like he's got rights to you know what and who."

"Louisa wouldn't let him get away with anything," Jamie said.

"That's what you think. You don't know how yucky she gets."

"So what can I do about it?" he asked gloomily, wishing May hadn't called. Some things were best not known.

"They want me to go visit a friend," May said. "If you dropped by, maybe . . . ." She left it open for him to consider.

He considered. "I'll be right there," he said and left his schoolwork spread over his desk. In the parking lot, the car wouldn't start.

"Come on," he told it, working the ignition key and the gas pedal. "I know I didn't get you your tune-up, but don't take revenge today." The engine refused to turn over. Jamie got out, flipped up the hood and checked oil and water. The battery was new enough so he was pretty sure that wasn't the culprit. He applied all his auto mechanics expertise, dried the points and tried the engine again. The starter mechanism clicked futilely.

Cursing, Jamie gave up and got his old ten-speed down from the wall at the back of his father's rented garage. He pedaled off, gloveless, trusting the pulsing of his hot blood to keep him from getting frostbite in the below-zero weather on this gray afternoon. By pushing hard, the ride took only half an hour, but it seemed endless because he worried all the way that Louisa and Bozo had already locked into an embrace which his presence wouldn't unlock.

Jamie left the bike outside and flung open the Murphys' glass and metal storm door. "Where is she?" he gasped as May appeared.

"Shush," May hissed. "They're up in her bedroom."

"Already?" Jamie blanched.

"She's showing him her photograph album."

"Is the door open or closed?"

"Duh!" May rolled her eyes as if his stupidity was unbelievable. "Open, of course."

"That doesn't sound too bad."

"Not bad, huh? Right here in the kitchen, he talked about getting engaged before he went off to engineering school so he wouldn't have all that kind of 'stuff' on his mind and could concentrate on studying."

" 'All that kind of stuff?' He didn't say that!"

"I told you he was a Bozo," May said.

"What did Louisa answer?"

"She said she had to think about it."

Jamie sighed. All was not yet lost. "I'm glad you called me," he said.

"Duh," May said, once again using the expression of contempt she'd picked up at school recently.

They sneaked up the stairs, but near the top, Jamie's conscience made him step hard on a stair tread in warning, and he said aloud, "Hey, May, when are you going to teach me that game you were telling me about? Clue, was it?" A threadbare Oriental rug covered the landing at the top of the stairs where a window seat full of cushions caught his eyes.

"We could play right here."

That brought Louisa to the door of her bedroom. Her eyebrows were raised over steel-pointed eyes. "What are you doing here, Jamie?"

"Visiting."

"What happened to the schoolwork you have to make up?"

"I finished it," he lied—then added lamely, "some of it, enough anyway."

"I have company," she warned him. He thought with awe of Amazon women warriors, then decided Louisa's auburn hair and glinting blue eyes were more Viking than Amazon.

"Hey," he said. "May and I are just going to— Hey, you don't mind if I hang out here a while, do you?"

"Yes, I do. Why don't you and May go play your little games in the living room downstairs?" No question that she suspected his intentions.

"Sure." He tried to sell her a smile, but Louisa wasn't buying. She disappeared back into her room, shutting the door behind her.

May got out the game and set it down on the couch in the living room. She was on her second explanation of the rules before Jamie could pay attention to anything but the searing image of Louisa upstairs with Vince in a room with a bed. It would be better to be home tackling his English papers. At least, there he could accomplish something, while here he was helpless to do anything but suffer. He groaned and May took pity on him.

"Listen, Jamie." She leaned across the couch and rapped his forearm for his attention. "She won't do anything so bad. Just let him kiss her a little. Let's play Clue, huh?"

"Why'd you drag me over here if she's in no danger of getting seduced?"

"I don't know. I thought just in case." May sounded apologetic.

He considered leaving, but just then Louisa's brothers tumbled in and came up with such instant enthusiasm for playing Clue with him that he stayed put.

"You better watch out for May," Jeff said to him. "She always wins."

"That's because I don't spend the whole game arguing, and I try to remember who asked what," May said.

The game got underway in the middle of the living room floor, and Jamie put his mind to it. He didn't feel like doing those essays now anyway. What was the use of anything if Louisa was lost to him? May won the first game. Jamie won the second with a correct guess on the murder weapon, one turn before Jeff would have given it.

"No fair!" Jeff protested, his freckles fairly dilating. "He just guessed, and I had the room and the killer first."

"Beginner's luck," Jamie said. "That's the breaks, kid."

"No," May said. "Jamie won because he's smart, like me."

Jeff protested and began an insult-slinging battle with May. The yelling brought Louisa down the stairs. Jamie was relieved to see that she was fully clothed and too serene to have been engaged in anything as stimulating as sex.

"What's going on down here?" she demanded.

Jeff and May shouted at the same time while Jamie observed and Billy wiped a drippy nose with the back of his hand. Louisa commanded silence and allowed them each to state their case.

"Jeff's such a baby," May began. "When I lose at Risk or chess or cards, I don't scream and yell about it."

"That's 'cause you know how dumb you are, you turkey," Jeff said furiously.

"Up to your rooms until you can talk without insulting people," Louisa said. "Both of you, march."

Jamie was impressed by her authority when Jeff took his furnace face off at once and May stomped angrily up the stairs behind him.

"Now what about you, Billy?" Louisa asked. "What are you going to do with yourself this afternoon?"

"Watch TV, I guess," he said. "How long do they gotta stay in their rooms, Louisa?"

"An hour should do it. You can tell them when it's time to come out." She turned to Jamie and said coolly, "Sorry to deprive you of your playmates."

Recognizing his marching orders, he rose to go and said, "My regards to Vincent. Tell him I'm sorry I couldn't stick around to meet him."

Before she could answer, Vince Brunelli himself started down the stairs, leaving the sound of a toilet flushing behind him.

"Vince, you know Jamie?" Louisa asked.

"Hi," Vince said. His dark eyes beneath strongly drawn brows and wavy dark hair descended on Jamie like rocks.

"Hi," Jamie shot back, not to be outdone in brevity.

"Vince and I are going for a walk," Louisa said. She turned to Vince and added, "Jamie was just leaving."

"You a friend of the family or something?" Vince asked suspiciously.

"Sort of."

"I'll get my jacket and boots," Louisa announced. Vince

was already dressed for the outdoors in a down vest over a wool plaid shirt and combat boots.

"You better wear a hat and gloves, too," Vince advised.

"My head never gets cold."

"No arguments, Lou. Just do it. I'll give you the scientific explanation while we're walking."

Jamie waited to hear Louisa ask Vince who he thought he was ordering around, but she only said meekly, "I don't own a hat." Her hand went to the springy red hair that encircled her face like the ruff of an Eskimo's parka.

"No gloves, either?" Vince raised an eyebrow as if Louisa were a child trying to get away with something.

"I'll see what I can find." She went to the alcove beside the kitchen door where winter coats and sweaters hung on brass hooks and boots were tumbled together on the floor.

"What are you up to this afternoon, Billy boy?" Vince asked the child, who was sitting dejectedly at the kitchen table with his chin propped on his crossed arms.

"I got nobody to do anything with. Louisa sent Jeff to his room."

"She did? What for?"

"Because May and him were fighting."

Louisa returned with a red scarf and mittens in hand. "How's this, Vince? Satisfied that I'll be protected from the elements?"

The quizzical eyebrow went up again. "Red is not your color," he said.

"You're the only one who's going to see me," she pointed out.

"And don't I count? Don't you want to look nice for me?"

67

His teasing was so heavy it made Jamie angry on Louisa's behalf, but she just sighed and said, "Okay, okay. I'll see if I can find my father's blue plaid muffler."

"What about my little buddy here, Lou?" Vince asked as she turned away. "How about springing his brother so Billy can have some fun, too?"

"Jeff deserved the restriction I put on him," Louisa said quietly. She raised her head from her search in a cardboard box of hats and gloves to give Vince a dark look over her shoulder.

Vince shrugged, backing off from the warning in her gaze, and told Billy, "Well, I tried, kid."

"I'm going to watch TV," Billy said and slipped out of the room.

Vince had a smirk on his face as he remarked to Jamie, "She's one tough lady, my big red Lou."

Louisa stood up, plaid scarf in hand. "Vince, I've told you I hate it when you call me that."

"Hey, look at the temper showing! How about if I call you wildcat instead?"

Jamie thought of May's private name for Vince and decided it was apt. Vince was a Bozo as he took Louisa by the shoulders and smiled cockily down at her, saying, "I like you best in blue, Louisa. Come and give me a smile now, huh, baby?"

When the smile appeared on command, Jamie's heart caved in. Any minute now she'd flutter her lashes. He couldn't watch. "Have a good walk, you guys," he said making for the door.

"Yeah, nice meeting you, Jamie," Vince said. "Maybe we'll see you at the match tomorrow night."

68

"What match?"

"The big wrestling match in Albany. It'll be my last one ever unless I decide to keep on wrestling in college."

"Did you say tomorrow night? This Thursday, you mean?"

"Right."

Jamie's eyes went to Louisa. Did she remember about his gymnastics competition tomorrow night? She was busy zipping her jacket, not looking his way. What could he say? She'd probably forgotten her promise altogether, and even if he reminded her, she couldn't do anything about it. Vince's match was the one she'd have to attend.

Say something, he begged her silently, but all she said was, "Come on, Vince. Let's go for our walk."

Even in the bulky down jacket that matched her eyes, she looked small beside Vince as she linked arms with him to lead him out the kitchen door. If she liked feeling small, they were a well-matched couple, Jamie admitted to himself.

"See you," she said to him as he walked out the door first.

Gloomily, Jamie repossessed his bike and mounted it. She couldn't be at both Vince's wrestling match and his gymnastics meet, not on the same night. Undoubtedly, she'd just forgotten her promise to him. Why not? He was easily forgettable beside a guy like Vince Brunelli. Fool, to have imagined he could compete.

"Jamie!" May called from a window overhead.

"What now?" He looked up at her elfin face in despair.

"Don't feel so bad," May said. "She'll never marry him."

"How do you know?"

"I know her. She fell in love before and got soft as Silly Putty until she got used to him, but when she went back to acting like her usual bossy self, they broke up."

"You're sure of that now?" Jamie asked his ten-year-old oracle.

"Positive. I don't give it more than another few weeks."

Recklessly, Jamie ignored his doubts of May's wisdom and clutched at the hope she had thrown him. He needed something to hold onto as he pushed his pedals up hill and down, trying not to think about frostbite and the possibility of losing all his fingers to the numbing cold. So what if Louisa was bossy? He wouldn't mind having her direct him. He could always smile and do as he pleased—unless she was right. Was there something lacking in him that her bossiness didn't bother him? Maybe what he was looking for was a mother. But his own mother hadn't been bossy at all. She had lavished love on him and enveloped him in the warmth of her approval. Whatever he did was right in her eyes, and if he neglected to pick up his toys or wash his hands, one disappointed look from her sent him flying to remedy matters. No, Louisa wasn't like his mother, and besides, his feelings for her were too hot and hungry to be confused with any other kind of love. But his feelings for her didn't matter because she didn't return them. No doubt, she'd soon apologize and say she couldn't make the gymnastics meet. Despite May's prediction, things did not look good for him.

He entered the apartment breathless from the squeeze of cold and took a few minutes to soak his hands in a sink full of tepid water. He'd have to hustle to get dinner ready by six, when Jake was due home. As soon as his fingers began to tingle and he could move them, Jamie got busy.

The singer on the local radio station was wailing so loudly about how he couldn't stop loving his old gal that Jamie didn't hear the phone until it had been a ringing a while. The pleasant voice of his father's receptionist warned him that the doctor was running late. "He says to go ahead and eat, and he'll get something cold when he gets in. I'm sorry, honey." As if it were her fault!

"Hey, no problem, Mrs. Donovan," Jamie assured her. They chatted for a few minutes. Then Jamie hung up and dished himself out some of the one-pot meal he'd made from leftovers with a can of mushrooms and some wine thrown in to garnish the plain fare. He was glad he hadn't invested time in frying up green peppers and onions as he'd planned.

After eating, Jamie went to the parking lot to try his car again, but it wouldn't work. For lack of anything better to do, he walked to the tennis club and asked a bleary-eyed Maury to exchange a five-dollar bill for quarters.

"You sure put a lot of dough into those machines," Maury said.

"Yeah, I'm working on winning a prize."

"They give prizes?"

"Only worthless ones."

Maury coughed and said, "Everybody to his own poison." He doled out the quarters. "You wouldn't be interested in getting more hours on the desk here, would you, Jamie?"

"I don't know. Might be. You planning on leaving?"

"Yeah, but don't tell anybody yet, okay?"

"Sure. Thanks for the tip-off." Nice of the kid to let him know, Jamie thought.

A new computer game bulked clumsily next to the old familiar Pac Man. In a minute, Jamie was concentrating hard on an intergalactic shoot out. The reality of being lost in

71

space with hostile forces advancing on him at the speed of light was greater than anything else in his life. The eerie whines and beeps and burps made more healing music than had the wailing singer on the radio. He played until he had run out of quarters and the club was ready to close. Then he returned to the apartment to see if his father had gotten in yet. Jake was snoring in his chair with the newspaper across his lap. Jamie took the cold misery in the pit of his stomach to bed with him.

JAMIE DIDN'T SEE Louisa Thursday morning, the day of the meet. He did see his English teacher, who dripped acid as she asked how he was going to feel about failing to graduate in June. He winced and promised to reform. "I'll believe it when I see it. If I see it," she said. And he'd imagined she was a nice lady!

Louisa didn't mention the gymnastics competition when he saw her in the cafeteria sixth period. He couldn't bring himself to say anything for fear of being forced to hear her regrets. Instead, he told her about the new water pump his car had needed, a subject that didn't interest either of them much.

That night, he prepared for the meet by trying to excise everything but vaulting from his mind. Even though it was his first competition, he knew the importance of being psyched up to win, and he told himself that whether Louisa came to watch him or not, he had an obligation to the coach

who had chosen him, to the other members of the team—
and to himself.

When he walked out with the rest of his team in their
matching gymnastics pants and warm-up jackets, he felt a
sense of loneliness in the high hollow box of the brightly lit
gym. The stands, which had been folded out from the wall
for the spectators, were sparsely filled. Men's gymnastics rarely
drew big crowds. The few people present were likely to be
relatives or friends of the competitors, and Jamie had no rep-
resentative of either group tonight. Jake was at the hospital—
busy saving lives, no doubt—and Louisa was sure to be in
Albany at Vince's wrestling match. Maybe Jamie should have
reminded her of her promise, but seeing her squirm out of it
would have been miserable for them both. He hadn't reminded his father, either, for the same reason.

Gymnasts had started doing stretching exercises on the mats
under the basketball nets which had been folded up out of
the way. A member of the Shaker team was trying out the
rings, arm muscles bulging. Two of Jamie's teammates were
taking turns spotting each other on the horizontal bar. Jamie
wasn't in the first three events. His turn would come after
intermission on the parallel bars, the rings and in the vaulting. With his heart beating at a nice steady pace and only a
faint queasiness in his gut, he began loosening up his calf
muscles with leg stretches, ignoring the stands, pretending
that this was just a practice session. The extra adrenaline he'd
need would no doubt start pumping through him during intermission when he knew his turn was coming.

The national anthem brought audience and participants to
their feet. Jamie kept his back to the stands, determined not

74

to keep looking for her and hoping when he already knew it was hopeless. She was on her way to Albany, probably at the wrestling match by now. The announcer introduced the judges. Two were men, gym-teacher types with clipboards, tall beside the petite Ms. Kreszak who taught girls' gymnastics and who was the only official Jamie recognized.

Earl Conover, standing next to Jamie, groaned. "I knew I shouldn't 've eaten dessert. I feel like I'm going to upchuck."

"You won't. You'll be excellent," Jamie said. Earl was in the first three events: horizontal bar, floor exercise and side horse.

"I wouldn't be so nervous except my whole family's up there watching me, even my grandfather," Earl said.

"You're lucky," Jamie told him.

"Who's there for you?"

"Nobody," Jamie said, and tried to smile and shrug as if it didn't matter.

"You're the one who's lucky," Earl said, and then his name was called and he walked out to the bars.

"No flash bulb pictures, please. We don't want the gymnasts distracted," the announcer instructed the audience over the P.A. system as someone in the stands stood up to take a picture of Earl. The buzz of voices ceased. In the silence, Jamie glanced over his teammates. He had only a slight acquaintance with them. They were loners mostly, eager to hurry off after practice to whatever their other activities were. Not one of them had extended himself to Jamie, and Jamie had made no effort to make friends, either. Still, he was disappointed by his team's mediocre showing in the first half of the competition. So far, Shaker had scored more points.

The coach was a low-keyed man with a paunch and college-age sons. One of his sons had cerebral palsy and the other two had devoted their high school athletic careers to skiing and soccer, respectively. The coach had been a star gymnast in college, but if he had a need for vicarious achievement, he didn't show it. He never pitted the team members against anything but their own best performance. Even now, his advice to the four men competing in the last three events was not to go out and beat the pants off Shaker, but to concentrate on performing as perfect a routine as they could manage.

"Okay, Landes, you're up for the rings," the coach said. "Take a deep breath. Let it out slowly and make like a chimpanzee swinging through the trees."

He gave Jamie a lift up to mount the rings. Jamie went through a swinging move and completed his strength moves successfully. Next came a kip-up. He snapped his legs forward and upward, reaching for a straight up position above the rings, but overshot his balance and came back down, almost falling off. That had blown it as far as his score was concerned. Well, rings had never been his forte anyway. He finished quickly, came off and faced the judges.

Just then, he thought he heard his name being called. As he walked off, he looked toward the slatted seats and stopped in his tracks. There in the third row from the top was Louisa. May sat beside her, waving at him frantically. He went hot with delight. She had come. To see him and not Vince. He waved and took a step toward her, but was stopped by the bark of his outraged coach. "Landes, you crazy?"

Obediently, Jamie returned to the cluster of his teammates, but he couldn't stop grinning. Louisa was there—for him. Through the P.A., the agitated announcer reminded the audience that they must not distract the participants in any way. Louisa's face was red. Jamie stared at her as if she were a mirage that might disappear.

"Look at that guy!" Earl Conover said, bug-eyed at the performance of a Shaker man, an Oriental who flew weightlessly as if he didn't even need the rings to keep him airborne.

"Your girl came?" Jamie was asked by the amiable kid who had been a fatty in middle school but was weasel thin now.

"Yeah," Jamie said, believing as he answered that Louisa was his girl.

He bounced onto the mats when his turn came at the parallel bars and went through a smoother routine than any he'd ever before achieved. It won praise from his teammates, who clapped him on the back for bolstering their team total. Their showing was good enough in this second half of the competition to reduce the Shaker lead substantially. "Those two Korean guys from Shaker are practically pros," the ex-fatty, Steve Whittaker, complained.

"Go show them how to do it," Jamie encouraged him, and when Steve came back from his parallel bar work, Jamie shook his hand and said, "Outrageous, Steve. You were the best."

Finally the time had come for the long horse vault. Jamie squeezed his eyes shut and reached inside his own core for the power to be better than he had ever been before. Concentrating on his body, he tried out the spring board a few times, feeling as if he were made of wires instead of muscle and bone. What he'd always liked about vaulting was its speed.

Now he tensed with the knowledge that he had only seconds to be spectacular. He could take a second run, but he usually did no better the second time around. It was now or never for him.

The signal came. "Louisa," he whispered to himself. His feet took over. Running from sixty-five feet back, he hit the spring board right and got a soaring lift. He could feel the height. Barely touching the horse for his handspring, he landed solidly with knees bent and arms out. He straightened up to face the judges and waited with wildly beating heart. No need even to think about a second vault. He'd outdone himself.

As he walked away, Jamie's eyes found Louisa in the applauding crowd. She was on her feet clapping for him, her face crimson with excitement. His girl! She had seen him at his best. He received the congratulations of his teammates, the laying on of hands that was ritual in victory or defeat, in a daze, unable to think of anything but the wonder of her being there as a witness, being there for him tonight.

Already the shorter, more wiry of the two Koreans on the Shaker team had hit the spring board. Jamie's eyes widened as the kid sailed through the air with incredible grace, a twist, a cartwheel and a perfect postflight landing. The crowd exploded. They'd never seen a high school gymnastics performance like this.

Jamie's team returned to their locker room, subdued, at the end of the meet. Shaker had won. Jamie was the only one still exhilarated.

"Listen, we were outrageous," he insisted. "So those Korean guys are Olympic material, but we were excellent."

"Yeah, well, better luck next time," Steve said glumly. Earl hunched into himself and told Jamie to go do something obscene to himself. The coach told them soberly that they'd put on a really good show and he was proud of them, but nobody except Jamie looked proud. He showered hurriedly and dressed, eager to get out to Louisa and May.

"Nice job, Landes," the coach said, and slapped Jamie's back as Jamie walked by him with his gym bag. "You really took off tonight. Too bad you got beat."

"Yeah," Jamie said. "Thanks." He gave the coach a smile and detoured over to where the Shaker team was dressing to shake hands with the Korean gymnast.

"Excellent vaulting, the best I've seen off TV," Jamie said.

The Korean smiled shyly and murmured a compliment in return. Finally, Jamie was free to find her.

Louisa was standing in front of the trophy case near the gym doors, reddish hair haloing her face above the bulky jacket, cheeks curved by a smile as she saw him coming. His girl, his big, bossy beauty!

"You were excellent, Jamie," she said and hugged him. "I had no idea you were such a terrific gymnast."

"You should have won," May said angrily. "That Shaker guy wasn't half as good as you."

"He was better," Jamie said.

"You looked perfect to me," Louisa said.

"It wasn't fair," May insisted.

"It was fair and I'm satisfied," Jamie said. "Boy, when I looked up and saw you in the stands, I was so happy I felt like flying."

"Well, you did. You flew," Louisa said.

Jamie held her hand. "Hey, you know, the least I can do for my fans is treat to sundaes at Friendly's. Okay?"

"That would be nice, but we have a ride waiting outside," Louisa said.

"So tell them to go on and I'll take you home." He felt so full of self-confidence that it didn't surprise him when Louisa promptly followed his suggestion.

Snowflakes, illuminated by the lights around the parking lot, flew at them as they walked to Jamie's car. He loved the snow at any time, but tonight, with Louisa beside him and his pride at his own achievement in the vaulting inside him, the snow was like confetti on a victory parade.

"So what's with Vince?" Jamie had the courage to ask. "Didn't he have a wrestling match tonight?"

"Uh-huh," Louisa said.

"But you came to see me instead?" Jamie pushed it.

She gave him a puzzled look and said cautiously, "Well, I'd promised you first, Jamie. I don't go back on my promises."

Her answer knocked him cold. All at once, weariness overcame him. Where had his head been? Of course, she hadn't come to see him because she cared more for him than for Vince, but only because she'd promised. She was a girl with principles. He should have known.

"What's wrong?" Louisa asked.

"Nothing," he said.

"Anyway," May put in, "you were super fantastic and I think those judges were dense."

He squeezed May's hand absently. He was only Louisa's friend, not her guy. Vince was her guy. "Jackass," came his father's voice in his head. Jackass to imagine anything more.

"You're so quiet all of a sudden," Louisa said in the car. They were in the front seat with May between them.

"Just a little tired," he said.

May started telling him how she had lost Glorious just before she and Louisa were to be picked up and taken to the meet tonight, and they almost hadn't been able to come. Then the guinea pig had emerged from underneath the couch, making them only a little late, but their ride had shown up even later.

Slowly, Jamie's spirits revived. Even if Louisa hadn't come for the right reason, she had come, and he might as well make the best of the evening. He parked in the lot next to Friendly's, put an arm around each sister and hugged them as they scuffed together through the inch of soft snow on the ground. May's head almost fitted under his armpit, and Jamie teased her. "Watch out you don't get lost down there."

"Duh!" she said.

They were lucky not to have to wait for a booth. As they walked in, the last one near the back became available. May asked if she could order a triple treat, and over Louisa's protest that that was too expensive, Jamie said, "Of course, you can have anything you want. We're celebrating tonight."

A waitress with a long black braid and freckles took their orders, a dish of sherbet for Louisa and a banana split for Jamie.

"So besides the temporary disappearance of Glorious, what else is new at the Murphy house?" Jamie asked when the waitress left.

"Nothing much," Louisa said.

"Except Vince's mad at Louisa for going to see you to-night," May said. "Louisa may have a problem because—"

"May Murphy!" Louisa warned. "What did I tell you about my private business?"

"But I thought if Vince wasn't going to take you to that movie—"

"SHUT UP!" Louisa said. May sank in her seat until she was resting on her own shoulders.

Louisa swept her hair back, refusing to meet Jamie's eyes. Silence stuffed the air between them. Finally their order came. Jamie eyed Louisa's raspberry sherbet and asked, "You dieting again?"

"Trying," Louisa said.

"Just for the record," Jamie offered, "I think you are a beautifully proportioned female."

"You're sweet, Jamie."

"So why don't you have a sundae tonight?"

"No, thanks."

"Doesn't my thinking you're beautiful matter at all?"

"Of course it does. Just it matters more how I feel about myself. You know that."

"I do?"

"Sure. You were proud of what you accomplished tonight even though you lost, right?"

"I guess so." Mostly he had been proud because she had been there, but he didn't want to pressure her by saying that.

"So I'll stay on my diet."

She was suffering, he realized, and not from excess weight, but because she'd fought with Vince. "Is there anything I can do to make Vince understand about your promise to me?" Jamie asked.

Louisa turned the spoon around and around in the middle of her sherbet. "He'll get over it," she said finally, but her eyes were suspiciously shiny when she smiled at Jamie.

"Really a serious fight, huh?" He felt guilty.

"No," she said, "it wasn't. . . . How's your ice cream, May?"

"Delicious." May was making it last, tasting each of the three flavors with their different toppings in tiny bites. Jamie had almost finished his split, but the girls had full dishes in front of them.

"Give me a taste, May?" he asked.

"Don't eat the cherry and don't take all the nuts," May said, reluctantly shoving her dish toward him.

"Generous little kid," Jamie teased, but all he sampled was some butterscotch that had leaked over the side of the dish.

Louisa asked him if he'd done any skiing yet this year.

"Not yet. You?"

"Vince was going to take me this weekend. Looks as if the weather will be right for it."

"I'll take you if he doesn't."

"No, thanks," Louisa said and switched subjects again. "What did Ms. Stetler say about your overdue work?"

Jamie entertained them with a dramatic reenactment of his exchange with Ms. Stetler.

"Won't your father be upset?" Louisa asked.

"Yeah, if I haven't worked something out by the time he finds out. I stuck the warning notice from English under a pile of advertisements and bills. He hasn't gotten to the bottom for a month. Besides, we don't see each other much lately, so I'm safe."

"I don't know why you don't just sit down and do the

work," Louisa said. "You're certainly smart enough to do it if you'd only get started."

"I'm glad someone has a good opinion of me," he said. "Stetler used to think I was cute, too, until I got behind. That lady really takes her job seriously."

"She's a good teacher, and you are cute, but you ought to cooperate with her."

"Okay," he said, pleased by her concern. "I will. This weekend. Promise." He held his hand up in the Scout's oath.

She still had half a dish of sherbet when she excused herself to go to the ladies' room. She wanted her sister to come with her, but May was still eking out her ice cream.

As soon as Louisa walked away, May said, "They had the worst fight, Jamie. I never saw Louisa cry so hard. Vince said if she went to your thing tonight, he was through with her."

"You think he meant it?"

"How should I know? But what I wanted to tell you is about tomorrow night."

"What are you telling Jamie now?" Louisa demanded.

"How did you get back so fast?" May said.

"There's someone in there. I can wait until we get home, and besides, I don't trust you out of my sight anymore."

"She was just telling me about Glorious's love life," Jamie lied.

"Glorious doesn't have a love life," Louisa said.

"She could if I could get her a male guinea pig," May said promptly.

On the drive home, Louisa started talking about the big Valentine's Day dance next week. Class officers were expected to attend, and besides, Louisa was on the decorations committee. This year, there were grandiose plans for constructing a tunnel of love and a wishing well and a great heart trimmed with paper flowers where couples could stand and get their pictures taken.

"Have you asked anyone to go with you?" Louisa asked Jamie.

"Not yet. You going with Vince?"

He held his breath hoping she'd sound doubtful, but without hesitation she said, "I expect to."

Jamie decided the fight couldn't have been as serious as May claimed.

By the time they arrived at the Murphy house, three inches of snow covered the road and falling flakes continued to smother the landscape. Louisa worried out loud about his driving back home, but he assured her his snow tires were in good shape and so was he.

"I know," she said and leaned across May to kiss his cheek. "I really admired your attitude tonight, Jamie. You *are* a winner." He reached for her, but she slid out the car door and headed for the house calling, "Thanks for the ice cream."

"Thank *you* for coming," he yelled after her.

"I'll call you," May said, and slid out the door after her sister.

The blizzard was worse going back. Snowflakes assaulted his windshield faster than his wipers could subdue them. Still, he felt good. Vince might have more points, but he hadn't won the meet yet.

*   *   *   *

Jamie realized that he had lost his house key only when he stood in front of his door fumbling in his pockets for it. Changing his clothes in the locker room after the meet—that was when he must have dropped the key. He went through

85

his gym bag, but couldn't find it. No matter. His father should be home, still reading or watching the eleven o'clock news.

Jamie rang the bell. He listened and thought he could hear the local newscaster's sonorous voice announcing the day's mishaps. He rang again, held his finger on the button. Jake hated that. Still nothing. Maybe his father had fallen asleep in his chair. He often did. Jake worked too hard, even though he'd never admit it.

Jamie considered. He was tired himself, full of muscle aches from the performance. He could walk over to the tennis club and call his father. Jake was trained to wake instantly at the ring of a phone. Wearily, Jamie trudged through the enveloping snow—at least four inches on the ground now. It silenced the world, insulated everything with loneliness.

Maury was just pulling on his jacket to go home as Jamie walked in. "Hi. Forgot my house key. Do you mind if I use the phone to call my dad?" Jamie said.

"Be my guest," Maury said. "Just shut the door behind you when you leave and turn the lights out, huh? Roads bad?"

"Getting there."

Maury waved and took off. Jamie reached for the phone, then looked at the comfortable leather couches in the center of the lobby on either side of a table stacked with tennis magazines. He could let his father sleep and zonk out here for the night if he could improvise some blankets. With the heat turned down for the night, it was too cold to sleep without a covering. He remembered that the towels were now kept under the desk; members had to pay a towel fee to the desk clerk to get one. Sure enough, there was a full laundry basket of clean towels, plenty to keep him warm if he layered them and didn't move around much. In the morning, he'd get home before his father left for work and maybe get a grunt of commendation from Jake for being considerate. Falling asleep on the couch was easy. All Jamie had to do was shut his eyes.

He woke up shivering early the next morning, yawned, folded his bed gear neatly back into place and left. The snow flowed undisturbed and luminous in the early morning light. Every step broke virgin whiteness. Jamie admired the shoulder pads on the tree branches and the helmets on the bushes. Even the severe lines of the apartments' gray wood siding were trimmed in white. He'd always liked the way snow transformed the world. He played a tattoo on the doorbell and waited.

An instant later, the door swung open and there stood Jake, wild-eyed and dressed in what looked like last night's rumpled clothes. "Where the hell have you been?"

"Sleeping at the tennis club, Dad."

"What kind of cockamamie story is that?"

"I couldn't wake you up when I got home last night, so I sacked out on a couch at the club. You fall asleep in front of the TV?"

"Why didn't you let yourself in?"

"Lost my key."

"I'll bet. Now tell me another. Where were you last night?"

The blood left Jamie's face. Sick to his stomach, he said quietly, "I just told you."

"Were you out drinking?"

Jamie looked into his father's furious face with disbelief. "I was at the gymnastics meet, remember?"

Jake did, suddenly. His cheek twitched though he gave no other sign. "And afterward?"

"Afterward I took some friends for ice cream and drove them home."

"You jackass," his father snarled in a backwash of anxiety, "why can't you ever remember your key? Where did you lose it this time?" Without waiting for an answer, he stood aside to let Jamie in and walked stoop-shouldered to his room as if the night had been hard on him, too.

Jamie went to the kitchen, but he wasn't hungry when he got there. He sat down at the table with a glass of juice and listened to the shower running. Jake hadn't even asked how the meet had gone. Just as well. Jamie would have hated to admit to his father that he'd lost. This morning, it seemed clear that he had.

◄8►

JAKE HAD LEFT for work with barely a good-by to Jamie, who sat alone in the kitchen making himself eat a bowl of cereal. When the phone rang, Jamie expected the call to be for his father. It was just past seven.

"It's me. Can you hear me?" a voice whispered.

"Almost," Jamie said.

"What I was trying to tell you last night," May said more loudly, "is Louisa promised to take my brothers to a movie tonight. See, she wants them to stop using the ice slide they made because it goes around a tree onto the pond, and she's scared they'll kill themselves. My father looked at it, but all he said was they should be careful. He hasn't seen how they whiz around in those space saucers."

"Uh-huh," Jamie said. "Very interesting, May, but how come you're telling me all this at just past dawn on a school day?"

"Because they picked a horror movie and she's got to take them."

"Is that supposed to mean something to me?"

"Well, Louisa is scared stiff of horror shows, and now Vince's not going and she has to go alone, and it's about werewolves. Yuck, gruesome!"

"Now I get it," Jamie said.

"Duh!" May answered.

"At the mall? Is the movie at the mall?"

"Look in the paper, why don't you?"

He thanked her and told her what a great little sister she was, to which she answered, "I've gotta go now," and hung up. He considered calling Louisa to offer her escort service, but realized that would expose May's clandestine maneuvering. He wasn't about to betray his only ally. Suppose he just showed up at the movie? It was worth a try, even though he couldn't imagine Louisa scared of anything. He'd be there for her to clutch, though, if she really was. Jamie whistled all the way to school.

*   *   *   *

The movie began at seven. At six-thirty, Jamie stationed himself inside the theater at the popcorn stand where his presence would seem accidental. The pretty girl behind the counter smiled at him as she handed him the warm container of buttered popcorn. "How's the movie?" he asked her.

"Awful," she said. "Lots of people scream and a kid threw up last performance."

"Not your thing?" He leaned an elbow on the counter and turned so he could watch the entrance, meanwhile offering the girl his popcorn.

"Ugh," she said. "I've gotten to hate that stuff as much as horror movies now."

"Right," Jamie said. "Sorry." He felt old watching the kids swarm in, mostly boys under fifteen. "Don't girls like horror shows?" he asked his candy counter acquaintance.

"Girls are too smart to pay to be scared," she said.

It occurred to Jamie that he had no appetite for horror movies, either. Only the chance to hold Louisa's hand had lured him here tonight, and where was she? At seven, Louisa still hadn't arrived. Jamie kept waiting.

In between sales, the girl told him she attended a community college where she studied dance and had just broken up with her boyfriend. The state university had a dance program next week that she wanted to attend, she said, and looked significantly at Jamie as she asked him, "Do you like to watch dancing?"

He had said he was waiting for someone, but he hadn't specified sex. Now he said, "My girl friend's the one who likes dance." The lie was a way of putting the girl off gently. She was pretty and nice but no more than a shadow beside Louisa's substance.

"I didn't know you liked horror movies," Louisa said at his elbow. Her brothers were already heading for the door into the darkened theater.

"Actually, I'm into werewolves. Considering changing my personality," Jamie said.

"Don't make me sick before the movie even starts," Louisa said.

Billy, usually the shyer brother, darted back to confide excitedly to Jamie. "My friend saw the show. He says the neatest part is when this guy's face begins to—"

91

Louisa clapped her hand over Billy's mouth. "Shut up or I'll take you home right now."

She did look paler than usual, Jamie noted with satisfaction.

"Hurry up, you guys," Jeff said. "Or we won't get good seats."

"Want me to sit with you, Louisa?" Jamie asked solicitously, offering Billy his popcorn box at the same time so that he wouldn't have to meet her eye.

"Would you, Jamie?" Louisa sounded grateful. "I may need someone to hold onto."

"Hey, Jamie," Jeff said. "I'll hold your popcorn while you hold my sister." His freckles lit up mischievously.

"It's a deal." Jamie sacrificed the popcorn box gladly.

Once inside, the brothers saw some friends in the front row and asked Louisa for permission to sit with them. She gave it.

"We could leave them here and go watch the comedy next door," Jamie suggested as he stood beside her in the back of the dusky room filled with kids who were squirming in their seats, crackling candy wrappers and spilling popcorn and soda over the floor.

"Can't," she said. "They're nowhere as tough as they like to pretend, and if they're going to have nightmares, I better know what about." She slipped her arm through Jamie's. "I'll close my eyes at the bad parts and you can tell me what happened afterward."

He didn't tell her he was likely to close his eyes, too. It felt too good to play the macho male in front of her for a change. They sat down where most of the empty seats were, in the back against the side wall.

92

"Want something to eat?" Jamie asked, squeezing her firm hand in his.

"Eat?" she groaned. "Don't mention food. My stomach is so shaky the popcorn smell is making me nauseous."

"You're a good sister," he said.

"I'm crazy," she answered. "I should have just told them I was too chicken to come and paid them off some other way. This is their reward for not breaking their necks on an ice slide they built down to the pond."

"I know," Jamie said incautiously.

"You know?"

"How dangerous that slide is," Jamie invented quickly to cover for May. Louisa looked suspicious.

"You're not even a little scared, are you?" she asked.

"It's just a movie," he said. "Real life's scarier than any movie."

"Not for me. Give me reality any day," she said. "Oh, how I wish this show was over. It's worse than going to have a tooth drilled. . . . Jamie, who was that girl at the popcorn stand?"

"Just a girl. She goes to a community college and takes dance."

"Isn't she a little old for you?"

"Hey," he said. "Do I run your love life?"

"Maybe you should. I'm making a mess of it myself."

"Fighting with Vince again?"

"He thinks I'm too involved with—other people."

"So what are you going to do?" Jamie asked.

"Nothing. He'll come around to seeing it my way soon."

"How can you be sure of that?"

"Because I know I'm right," she said. "He's acting stupid."

The canned music cut out. Louisa's eyes widened as she fixed her attention on the screen where an open window and a stormy night set the scene suspensefully. In front of the window and behind the credits was a woman's head. Outside the window, the trees made suggestive shapes around the bright orb of the moon. Louisa screamed and squeezed her eyes shut and dove for Jamie's shoulder before the credits had even run out.

Jamie rated it the most enjoyable movie of his life. Not that he saw any of it. He was too busy attending to Louisa. She peered at the dread-inducing scenes from the safety of his encircling arms or out of the corner of one eye while Jamie buried his nose in her hair, sniffed languorously of the lemony scent and got tickled by her soft, springy curls. The pressure of her body against his thrilled him, and when the young man in the movie turned into a werewolf before their eyes, and Louisa squealed and hid her head against his shoulder, he came near to ecstasy. Unrebuked, he stroked her back and kissed her hair. She only withdrew at moments when the screen released her from its highs of horror, and then she sat tensely, eyes forward, hand still in his, ready to dive for cover at the next macabre happening. Her milky skin was luminous in the dark, and he could admire the adorable uptilt of her nose at his leisure. His big, beautiful girl! If only the horror show would continue forever and his competition die of old age out there in the real world.

The end of the movie afforded Jamie one last contact with a trembling Louisa when the werewolf was consumed by the fiery inferno of the mad scientist's mansion. Then the lights came on. His hour-and-a-half sampling of heaven was over.

94

Louisa looked exhausted. "Awful," she said. "Sick and aw-ful. How could you stand it, Jamie?"

"Easy," he said, not bothering to explain that he hadn't watched the show at all.

"Those stupid kids," she said. "I bet they're wishing they'd picked a Walt Disney special. Let's go see if they're okay."

He offered her his hand, but she was herself again and didn't take it. "There they are," she said. The boys looked undamaged as they hiked up the aisle toward them in the crowd of exiting kids.

"Can we go to Flavorland with our friends, Louisa?" Jeff asked. "We've got our own money."

"Eat? You're going to eat after seeing all that gruesome stuff?" Louisa asked.

"Please, Lou. We won't take long. You and Jamie could come, too."

"No, thanks," Louisa said. "My stomach won't settle down for a week."

"We could sit in the mall and wait for them," Jamie sug-gested. "We could sit next to the fountain. That'll soothe your fevered brain."

"My brain's not fevered; it's permanently damaged by that weird show, but okay. You kids look for us there when you're done."

To make his bliss complete, she thanked him as they walked out of the theater together. "You don't know how much I appreciate your sitting with me, Jamie. It was lucky for me you were there. And you were going to sit through that show alone?"

"Well, sure," he said, and made a private vow never to

admit that horror shows gave him nightmares.

The fountain in the middle of the mall was set in an imitation park sunk below floor level with real trees in large pots and houseplants in planters separating park benches. The splashing water, the greenery and the isolation gave the illusion of peace and privacy. Usually, seats were hard to come by because teenagers hung out here as well as weary shoppers with packages and mothers with babies in strollers, but tonight they shared the place only with a couple affixed to each other in what looked like a permanent embrace.

"How about an orange drink?" Jamie asked. He had glimpsed the top of the stand through the tree in front of him.

"No, thanks," she said, "but you get one if you want."

"I'm not thirsty. Did Vince forgive you for going to my meet instead of his last night?"

"We discussed it," she said briefly.

"He's still mad, then?"

"He thinks I'm rigid. Don't *you* feel guilty about last night, Jamie. He's got to learn that I'm not always going to do the things he wants."

"He's a pretty solid guy, though, isn't he?" Jamie asked in the hope of uncovering further flaws in invincible Vincent.

"Oh, he's great, as solid as they come. Only he sees everything from one point of view—his own. Nothing in my life can be as important to me as he is—he thinks. Well, my life is full of things that are important to me, and he's got to realize I need freedom to be myself. I'm not just his girl."

"He sounds self-centered," Jamie said.

"'I guess you could say that."

"But you like him anyway."

96

"Well, he's loaded with other good qualities."

"Yeah," Jamie admitted.

"And, of course, he's mature enough to know what he wants out of life, and he's going to get it, too."

Jamie knew what he wanted out of life, but nobody had ever judged him especially mature. "You think goals make the man, Louisa?"

She thought about it. "I guess I do—in a way—think goals define who you are. That's what shakes me up so much about myself, that I can't pick a direction. You have to wonder what's wrong with a girl who can't decide whether she wants to reorganize the social system or to get married and have a big farm and raise ten children." She sighed. "Then to confuse myself even further, I also make claims to wanting to be a potter. It's insane to want to go in such different directions."

"Not if you did them one at a time," Jamie said.

She laughed. "I'm not superwoman even though you think so."

"Don't kid me," he said. "I know your secret identity."

Her face shone with the flush of his compliment as she said, "What do you want out of life, Jamie?"

"I can't tell you."

"Why not?"

"Because you'll think I'm a fool."

"Never," she said. "I think of you as a very strong person—the things you've overcome, the drugs and the drinking and your mother's leaving you." She touched his cheek. "Why, you can even sit through horror movies without flinching."

"Am I as strong as Vince?"

97

"In a different way. You get knocked down and come back. You're resilient. That's a kind of strength."

He wondered if resilient was as good as solid, or just second best. He didn't want to be second best. He'd loved his mother, and it had nearly killed him to discover that he wasn't first with her. He loved his father, but he wasn't even sure his father liked him. He loved Louisa and she loved Vince. If that didn't make him a fool, it sure came close.

Louisa squeezed his hand. "You're such a good friend, Jamie," she said. "I don't have anybody I can talk to the way I can with you."

"Lousia," Jeff called from the stone steps on the store level of the mall. "We're done."

"Do you have transportation?" Jamie asked her.

"Sure. I have my mother's car. Do you need a lift?"

He didn't, but he saw no reason why he shouldn't leave his car in the parking lot and let Lousia drop him off. She had to drive by his place anyway, and he could spend a few more minutes beside her and hitch back to pick up his car tomorrow. Even though he was just her good friend, he had held her in his arms tonight. It was an evening he was in no hurry to end.

*   *   *   *

The thunderous chords of Beethoven's Fifth meant Jake was home. Jamie hung his jacket in the hall closet and sauntered into the living room, still high on the pleasure of his evening with Louisa. One glimpse of his father's murderous expression brought him down fast. "Something wrong, Dad?"

"I've been waiting up for you," Jake said grimly. He stood near the window with his arms laced shut across his chest.

98

"I'm not late, just went to a movie with a girl, Louisa Murphy. Great movie, all about a werewolf."

"Just the kind of asinine entertainment you would appreciate."

"Hey, what's the matter? Did you hear I robbed a bank or something?"

"Cut the wise remarks, Jamie, and sit down." Jake strode past him to switch off the stereo unit. Jamie lowered himself into a brown leather armchair and picked up the Eskimo walrus carving from the glass table beside him for the solace of stroking its smooth back.

"Put that down," his father snapped.

"Somebody go and die on you today?" Jamie asked. All that ire couldn't be from anything he'd done, but sure as he was of his own innocence, he felt guilty. Resentfully, he waited to hear what crime he was supposed to have committed.

"What I can't understand," Jake rumbled into the silence, "is how any son of mine could be so damn feckless."

"Dad, I have to tell you, I don't have a clue to what's bothering you."

"You don't? Cut the crap and tell me what you're into now, Jamie. First dope, then booze. What are you using now to assist you in shirking your responsibilities?"

"What'd I do, forget to take out the garbage?"

"And you better cut the sarcasm along with the wise remarks."

"My behavior has been Boy Scout perfect for a year," Jamie said. "I'm clean. Whatever you think I've been doing, you're wrong."

"It's what you're not doing. I walked into your room to-

99

night expecting to find you in it because you had neglected to turn your tape deck off—as usual."

"That's only the second time in a month—"

"I'm not finished. . . . And when I didn't find you in your room, I looked around for a clue to where you'd gone. A note, an arrow pointing east, something."

Jamie took a deep breath. He could have, but didn't, point out that Jake frequently left no word of his whereabouts either. No matter. His father could claim he was always either in his office or at the hospital. On the other hand, Jamie was pretty used to coming and going unremarked in the empty apartment. How was he supposed to know his father would be home tonight?

"What I found on your desk was the pile of applications, college applications, pristine as the day they arrived. Would you care to tell me what colleges you've applied to so far?"

Jamie shrugged, anger stirring sluggishly within him.

"You do realize that it's February?" Jake said.

"Yes."

"What was all the bull about wanting to become a doctor? Change your mind?"

"No."

"Then explain to me how, in that whiz bang brain of yours, you expect to make it to medical school if you don't even get into college in the first place? Or have those idiotic video games you devote yourself to addled you so badly you didn't realize there was a sequence involved?"

"Don't worry about it," Jamie muttered, fighting to control his temper under the barrage of verbal slaps.

"I'm not going to worry about it, but I'm going to warn

100

you. If you don't manage to get yourself accepted at a repu-
table college for next fall, I'm kicking your butt out of this
place. I don't expect to support a ne'er-do-well." His father's
voice had risen to a roar.

"I hear you, Dad."

"And what are you going to do about it?"

"I was planning to get the applications done."

"Were you? And what has kept you from doing them for
the past four months? Do you think the admissions offices
are waiting with bated breath to hear from you? A mediocre
student with neither academic drive nor outside interests to
show for four years of high school?"

"My SAT scores were pretty high."

"Just remember, you're not going to be a parasite. You're
going to earn your own way. I'm not handing you anything
on a silver platter just because you're my son."

"I'm sorry I'm such a big disappointment to you," Jamie
said, keeping his voice low. "I can't help not being as smart
as you are. I've done my best—"

"You haven't. Your best wouldn't leave you time to run
around playing stupid games and entertaining yourself with
horror shows. Your best would mean cracking the books and
studying hard. You've never done anything hard in your life."

Jamie stood up. The rage that he'd been suppressing scalded
the moisture in his eyes. "Thanks a lot, Dad," he said.

He turned and headed for his room, shut and locked the
door behind him, then threw himself face down on the bed
and punched the pillow helplessly. His father despised him.
His father considered him a parasite. All the efforts he'd made
to please the bastard—trying to keep the household going,

101

trying to be cheerful and to keep the bastard company in case he might be lonely, and now he was a parasite. Didn't the bastard know how hard it was to kick bad habits? Didn't he know what it had cost Jamie to turn his back on those drinking companions who offered good-buddy warmth and easy laughter? So he was a parasite. No way could he please Jake. No way could he ever win with Dr. Landes.

"Jamie, come out here," the angry voice outside his door commanded.

"Leave me alone."

"Not until I finish talking to you."

"I've finished listening."

Jake pounded on the door. Jamie got up and yanked it open. Damned if he was going to act scared. "I got your message loud and clear," Jamie said.

Fury distorted his father's face. Here was the real horror movie. Jake was going to hit him, wanted to so badly Jamie flinched from the coming blow, but nothing happened. The engorged face subsided to its normal heavyset grimness.

"You are my son," Jake said. "I just don't want you to waste your life." Then he turned and shambled off to the kitchen where no doubt the shot of Scotch would calm his nerves. Jamie wished he had recourse to the same medicine.

Instead, he took a long, hot shower and got into bed with the curtains open so he could look out at the stars. All he could see was sifting snow. White flakes dotted the halo of light from the street lamp. Time was cocooned in white full of unborn secrets, and the only movement was the snow slanting down in hurrying, pin-sized flakes.

Useless. Useless to even live when your own father hated

you. What was the point if nobody cared? All he had was himself. Suppose all he ever had was himself? Louisa. Her face glowed like a cameo in his mind's eye, the sweet, clear profile he'd studied in the movie house, her softness pressing into him. He needed her so much. Shouldn't the force of his need make her respond to him? "Louisa," he whispered. "Why can't you see me as a man?"

The monotonous journey of the scurrying snowflakes failed to soothe him. He felt so far removed from sleep that he got up and dressed. Out in the hall, he could hear his father's heavy breathing. Jake hadn't had any trouble falling asleep. He'd dumped his anger. It was all on Jamie now.

Jamie walked into the snowstorm, heading for the club-house and the game room. If it was open, he could play a while, long enough to soften the rock in his chest. It was not quite eleven-thirty but the clubhouse door was already locked. The desk clerk could leave early if no courts were reserved for the last hour. Tonight he'd been lucky and Jamie was not.

Going back with the wind behind him, Jamie felt insulated in his down jacket, walled off by the spinning snowflakes which silenced even the car making slow black tracks on the road. Already, the world was sheeted in white, the pureness of it illuminated at intervals by the streetlamps along the curving drive. He could try Schenectady. An arcade he knew there was open all night.

In the parking lot, he realized he'd left his car at the mall so he could steal extra time with Louisa. Might as well go to bed. If he couldn't sleep, he could always try filling out an application. "Why do you want to come to this college? . . .

Describe your goals in life. . . . Write a five-hundred-word essay about yourself." He'd already filled up a wastebasket trying. Everything he wrote sounded either damning or dumb. They'd never let him into college on the basis of anything he said about himself. If he told the truth, they'd lock their doors against him—former dope addict and alky, presently pretty hopeless—and when he tried to make himself sound good, it always came out phony.

Lights were on in his apartment. Jamie hesitated, key in hand, dreading another confrontation. Then he unlocked the door. Let Jake hit him and get it over with. Without his car, Jamie's only escape was to curl up in a snowbank and he wasn't ready to die of exposure yet.

"Where were you?" Jake asked.

"Couldn't sleep, so I went for a walk."

Jake gave him a glazed stare. "In this weather?"

"Yeah."

"Well . . . better shut off the lights," Jake mumbled and turned to do it himself.

Jamie went to his room, shucked his clothes, got between his cold sheets and faced a colder question—did his father love him? Was Jake capable of loving a son in whom he had no pride? The snowflakes flew thicker and faster than ever. The question fell with them, unanswered, into the darkness of sleep.

◄9►

JAMIE COULD SMELL the morning coffee brewing in the automatic pot set to go on at six-thirty, and he could hear the clink of his father's iron egg pan on the electric range. In a few minutes Jake would have eaten his two eggs and an English muffin, finished his daily dose of the morning paper and gone. Jamie had awakened with his anger intact. He lay still in bed, waiting until he had the apartment to himself. The injustice of Jake's attack rankled. At the hospital, his father was known as a man without a temper, a man of endless patience. He had never lost his temper with his wife, either, as far as Jamie knew. Only Jake's son had the dubious distinction of bringing out the worst in him.

As soon as the front door clicked shut, Jamie got up and took a shower. He dressed in jeans and a wool shirt with rolled-up sleeves. Saturday. Hours ahead like cash in hand to spend. He stood at the window. The snow had stopped falling, leaving behind an all-white landscape against the blue

105

sky. Everything was quilted with snow except the vertical browns of tree trunks. He could go skiing alone. Always the chance of meeting someone on the slopes, somebody he could buddy up with for the day. Louisa was going skiing with Vince. Unless Vince was still angry with her. If Vince hadn't gone to the movie with her last night, he might not take her skiing today, and if they continued feuding, she might need another escort to the Valentine dance next Saturday. Class officers traditionally had to attend, and Louisa was not one to ignore tradition.

Jamie allowed himself to dream. He would lead her onto the dance floor, and people would stare with surprise, but no one would comment because the look in Louisa's eyes would tell them that Jamie was her new guy.

"I've never noticed what a good dancer you are," Louisa would say.

"You've never danced with me before."

"You're different in a lot of ways from what I thought. It's as if I never really knew you."

"I've always known you, Louisa, and loved you."

Their goodnight kiss would become a passionate embrace, and she would cling to him and whisper finally, "I love you, too, Jamie."

While he was waiting for it to be late enough to call Louisa, he started hiking toward the mall. He hadn't gotten two breaths of well-chilled air before a classmate on his way to work offered Jamie a ride, and half an hour later he was back home, hungry from the exertion of digging his car out of the snow in the parking lot at the mall. With wheels at his disposal again, he ate a couple of packaged doughnuts and drank the rest of the coffee, then dialed Louisa's number, even though it was only eight in the morning.

"What're you doing on this great winter day?" he greeted her cheerfully.

"Hi, Jamie. You're up early. I'm getting ready to go cross-country skiing with Vince."

"Oh, you and he made up?"

"Sure. We only had a little misunderstanding, nothing serious."

"Good," he said, sadly tossing out his dream. "Have fun then. . . . I suppose you're busy tonight, too?"

"Tonight I'm baby-sitting the boys and May so the folks can go meet some old friends for an annual reunion."

"Want me to come keep you company?"

"Vince's probably going to be here, and the truth is, he's getting a little jealous of you, of our relationship. He knows we're old friends, and I told him that I'm fond of you. So now—well, you understand."

"Don't say another word," Jamie said. "You've just made my day."

"How?" she asked. "What do you mean?"

"Never mind. I'll come over tomorrow. We could build a snowman maybe, you and me and the kids."

"Fine. That'd be fun," she agreed, and that was the end of their phone call.

The news that he'd made Vince jealous left Jamie feeling so powerful that he decided he would tackle the applications after all, tackle them and beat them into submission. He put his favorite tape on and adjusted the speakers so that when he sat at his desk, the music surrounded him. The husky-voiced singer told him about how good life was when the bowl was full and the game was there to be won. Jamie listened while he carefully inked in all the dates, numbers and names requested on the forms, using the penmanship techniques drilled into him by his third grade teacher. His handwriting was pretty good when he took his time, he noted—a little on the small and slanty side, but clear enough. Next came the hard part—the essays.

"Describe the values most important to you." He wrote quickly, "The values most important to me are honesty and consideration for others." Sunday school kiddish. He crossed that out, then erased the line and switched to scrap paper. Two strikes against him for a messed-up application form. Values—what did he believe in? Sticking by what you've promised, being a responsible person, leaving the world a better place than you found it. Values—working hard but enjoying life, too. What exactly did they mean by values?

He wrote, "I want to be a decent person respected by others and so I can respect myself. Like any decent person, I value—" He couldn't decide which one to choose, and this was the easy question. There were three others to answer on this application alone. "Who or what were the major influences on your life? What do you expect to be doing ten years from now? What do you consider are your accomplishments in life so far?"

He groaned and fidgeted, went to the kitchen and ate a piece of cheese, thought about what perfect skiing weather he was missing, and finally forced himself back to his desk. He turned off the tape deck, picked up his pen and quickly copied a series of values selected at random from the ones he'd noted on his scratch pad. He wasn't sure whether he was supposed to say why they mattered to him or not, but decided he'd spent enough time on that question.

The major influences on his life—his mother and father. "My mother hugged me a lot and told me what a great little kid I was. Since I respected her opinion, I believed her," Jamie wrote on his scratch pad. "Only when I grew up I realized that she probably just liked me because I am or was her son. My mother died when I was fifteen. Before she died, she left me, but at least she taught me how to enjoy my life. She enjoyed her life, too, mostly. The other big influence on my life has been my father. While I'm not like him at all, being medium height, medium looks, medium smart and medium athletic, I'd like to follow in his footsteps. He's a really dedicated doctor. I admire people who dedicate themselves to helping others, and that's what I'd like to do with my life."

If he weren't such a grand total of average! Maybe his mother had done too good a job of teaching him how important it is to enjoy life. If he were more like his father, he'd have studied harder, racked up a better average in high school, made some impact on the world already. What college wanted an average of nothing much in the candidates? Unless he lied, he couldn't make himself sound special. All he could say was that he was a nice guy, that he liked people. Good qualities for a doorman, a waiter or a salesman, but he wanted to be a doctor. He'd make a good pediatrician if he could get through medical school. But who was he kidding? He wasn't even going to make it into a college from which a medical school would accept him. Jake was right as always.

In disgust, Jamie ripped up his notes and dropped them into the straw wastebasket from Jamaica. They'd bought him the wastebasket in the straw market one morning on their way to the beach, his mother and Thomas. Jamie remembered the turquoise water that was clear right down to the white sand below it. Where the coral grew, gaudy fish swam like water butterflies, and under the golden sun there was plenty of time for a swim, a laugh, a listen. "Do you always have fun here?" Jamie had asked in wonder, and his mother had said, "People suffer here just like anyplace else, Jamie. Only they don't make a fetish of it like your father does." Would she have died anyway if she hadn't run away to Jamaica? Sooner maybe—inside. But she should have taken Jamie with her if his father was such an ogre. She should never have left her beloved son behind, not if she loved him as much as she said.

He looked with distaste at the empty spaces on the application forms, bottomless holes to fill with garbage. The thing to do was lie. He erased "honesty" as one of the values he held and began inventing some accomplishments for himself. "One of the things I'm proudest of is the peer drug counseling program which I initiated in our high school."

He wondered if they'd check to see if his high school had such a thing. It didn't. He'd suggested it two years ago to his guidance counselor, who told him the administration did not officially recognize any problem with drugs in their school. Jamie had then gone to his health science teacher, a young guy who knew what the score was. The health science teacher agreed it was a great idea and suggested that the way to get the school's approval was to work through Student Council.

Jamie had tried that and got the cold shoulder from the Student Council president, who didn't want to be tainted with anything to do with drugs.

Privately, Jamie had tried to offer friendly support to a kid he knew who was into amphetamines. The kid overdosed and died before they'd gotten very far, and Jamie gave up.

"I also am responsible for saving the life of a boy who fell through the ice while skating. I reached a hockey stick to him and flipped him up like a fish." Not a bad way to put it, Jamie thought, and besides, it was true. But it happened when he was thirteen, too long ago to count as an accomplishment on a college application. He wondered if returning the old lady he'd found wandering barefoot down the highway last year to the nursing home counted as an accomplishment. She'd told the nurse he was her grandson. That had tickled him so much that he went back to visit her, but she hadn't remembered him then, and when he said he was her grandson, she called him a liar. The experience had been humiliating, though he told it as a funny story on himself later.

He crossed out what he'd written, and on the application form under accomplishments he wrote, "None." Then he relented and added, "But I plan to do a lot with the rest of my life." There, let them make something of that.

He revised his notes on his mother and father under the question about who had influenced him, and resisted the urge to add Pac Man to the list. College admissions people probably didn't have much sense of humor, judging by the questions they asked.

He slipped the form in the envelope which he'd long ago addressed and stamped in an excess of efficiency. Sealing the envelope, he suddenly got depressed. Who was going to let him into college on the basis of what he'd written? What was the sense of trying to prove he was something special when he wasn't?

"Trash it," he told himself. "Louisa wouldn't like you so much if you were such a nothing." Or did she just feel sorry for him?

Waste of a day. He should have gone skiing. The snow looked so enticing, crystalline where the beams of sunlight shone on it through the blue tears in the clouds. With what was left of the afternoon, he could at least drive to the mall and get Louisa a valentine card, a funny one.

On the way to his car, he scooped up a handful of snow, packed it and threw a snowball at a tree. The snow was so perfect for building that he stooped and sculpted a miniature snowman. It was then that the idea hit him. Forget the paper valentine. Instead, he'd build one of snow for Louisa. Something original like that would impress her. And he wasn't going to win her away from his rival just by hanging around her doorstep wagging his tail. A bold gesture might do it. Why not risk it?

Charged with enthusiasm, Jamie returned to the apartment for gloves and a snow shovel, all the while considering likely spots to construct his masterpiece. The notion of building it right in front of the decorative brick wall that separated his apartment complex from the county road struck him as brilliant. Monday morning in the school bus on her way to school, she'd either see it or have it pointed out to her. Could anything prove the sincerity of his love more than to plant his heart right on the roadside for the whole world to see?

Jamie borrowed the maintenance man's wheelbarrow without any trouble. The heart would need a buttress behind it, a snow wedge to support the shape which must flare up from a narrow bottom to double curved wings at the top.

Energetically he set to work to mold the piles of snow which he carted from inside the wall where it was drifted deep and untouched. Wedge and heart grew upward together in a solid construction. At first he had a stubby four-foot-high sculpture in mind, but as he worked, his ambition grew, until by late afternoon he'd built a mammoth heart, six feet high with a ramp of snow behind it strong enough to hold his weight as he clambered up to perfect the uneven curve at the left top.

Already his heart had caused comment. A car full of seniors had driven by, then backed up so grinning faces could hang out the windows and call,

"Hey, Jamie, what are you advertising?"

"Lost your heart, Jamie?"

"Too cheap to buy a valentine, kid?"

"Up yours," he told them, laughing.

With the last dim light of the day, he stood on a stepladder and, using a garden trowel, carefully dug out letters on the smooth face of his heart. "Jamie loves Louisa." He didn't care who laughed at him. He wasn't ashamed of having the whole world know how he felt about her. And Vince would never be able to top this one.

Streetlights lit the dark as Jamie returned all the tools he'd borrowed and went home to make himself dinner. His father had been invited out tonight by an associate who probably wanted to introduce Jake to yet another lady whom he wouldn't make any time for in his life. What did the great Dr. Landes need human companionship and love for, so long as he had enough patients to keep him busy?

Jamie ate a can of tuna fish and a peanut butter sandwich. He was too tired from his afternoon's exertions even to heat himself a can of soup. Afterward he flopped on his bed to take a quick nap.

He only woke up when his father's voice asked, "You all right?" Jake stood at the open door of Jamie's bedroom. The clock said eleven.

"I'm fine," Jamie said. "Did you have a good time?"

"So so. You didn't go out?"

"I was working on the applications."

"Good, good. . . . Well, see you in the morning." Jake gave his shorthand smile and moved down the hall to his own bedroom.

Jamie undressed. Tomorrow was Sunday. He'd be seeing Louisa. He yawned and went back to sleep.

The freezing rain began sometime in the night. In the morning, the snow was coated with ice. Trees were sheathed in clear ice, each twig glittering separately in the bright sunshine. The ground looked like a skating rink in shades of gray and black and milky white depending on what was underneath the slick surface. Jamie's first thought was that it was just as well there'd be no snowman-building at the Murphys' since his body still ached from yesterday's labors. He wondered how his heart had withstood the weather change and hurried to get showered and dressed so he could get outside to look.

He was in the kitchen gulping milk from the container

when his father barked his name from the front door. Jamie jumped and spilled the milk. Jake was dressed in warm-up suit and green loden coat. Obviously he'd been on his way to his racquet ball game.

"What did you have to do with that monstrosity on the road out front?" Jake asked.

"The heart? I built it," Jamie said. "It's sort of a joke."

"Did you have to sign it?"

"It's still there, huh?"

"There? It's fixed in ice so thick that it won't melt until July. Who's Louisa?"

"She's a girl I know."

"Obviously you know her. The whole world knows you know her. Was it necessary to make such a public jackass out of yourself for her?"

"Hold it, Dad. I think you better cut the insults."

"Why? What's insulting about calling a jackass a jackass? You had me believing you'd spent yesterday knocking yourself out on those applications and what do I find you were doing? Playing in the snow like a little kid. You've made yourself a public laughingstock."

"What do you care? Nobody's going to laugh at you," Jamie said.

"I've had enough of your kindergarten behavior, Jamie. You either start acting more like an adult or move your butt out of here. I'm not going to put up with any more."

"You want me to move out? Okay, I will."

"Will you? Where would you go? You couldn't even earn your own milk money, let alone support yourself. Now go to your room and sit down and finish those applications." Jake had been yelling. He lowered his voice to add, "Furthermore, I want to see the finished papers before you've got permission to leave this house."

After the door slammed, Jamie put down the carton of milk which he was still gripping and mopped up what he'd spilled. Then he walked into his bedroom, got his suitcase out of the back of his closet and began packing.

‹10›

ALTHOUGH HE WAS acting without having made a conscious decision, Jamie had no question about the correctness of what he was doing. An automatic reaction made sense when there were no options. He had to leave. To stay after Jake's latest assault would be self-destructive. It would mean losing whatever self-respect he had.

Jamie concentrated on filling his suitcase with necessary essentials: clothing, toilet items, a transistor radio, his school books, his savings bank account book, and a couple of unread sci-fi paperbacks.

It wasn't until he drove out of the complex and saw his iced-over heart glittering like a roadside advertisement set to catch the motorists' eyes that he had misgivings. Then they were not about leaving his father, but about Louisa. It suddenly occurred to Jamie that the heart might embarrass her. He had built it on an impulse of affection, as a lark, as a free offering, but she'd made it plain that he was just her friend.

Her heart belonged to Vince. How would the Bozo see Jamie's roadside valentine? As a challenge, no doubt. It might even provide Vince with a good excuse to insist that Louisa stop seeing Jamie since, obviously, he was getting false ideas from his license to hang around her.

He'd made a foolish mistake, all right. Still, his father shouldn't have spoken to him with such utter contempt. Acting like a fool once in a while was normal at his age. He was adult enough and had graduated from kindergarten long ago, despite what Jake said.

As he drove toward Schenectady, Jamie decided to check in at the Y for tonight. Tomorrow, he'd take a day off from school and go find a job—any job that would pay him enough to live on and that was available immediately. There had to be something, probably something hard or dirty that nobody else wanted—a night job would be best. Then he could attend school by day. In any case, he had enough in his savings account to keep him going for a couple of weeks.

He thought about what a factory job on a night shift would be like. Was he tough enough for a grind like that? "Sure you are," he told himself. "You can do anything you have to do." The echo behind the reassurance was in his mother's voice. Her legacy was the faith he had in himself. It was, in truth, what had helped him get past the drugs and drinking and past the loneliness of cutting himself off from old associations. His father might consider him a loser, but Jamie wouldn't believe it, not yet, anyway. He drove carefully around the winter potholes, not thinking beyond getting to the YMCA across from the bus station.

According to the wasted-looking man at the desk, Jamie was lucky to find an available room. He paid in advance, took the key and was directed up the stairs and down the hall. The room was freshly painted, but curiously shabby, with a green iron bedstead, scarred wooden dresser, single straight-back chair and an accordion-pleated iron radiator unlike any heating device Jamie had ever seen. Beside the bed was a rickety night table with a scrawny lamp and over the bed hung a woeful picture of Christ on the cross. There was sure to be a Bible someplace, Jamie thought, but he couldn't find one. As soon as he got a job, he'd find a cheerier place to live. He opened his suitcase and spread some of his belongings around the room the way an animal claims territory by spraying it with his personal odor.

Tonight he'd call his father just to let Jake know where he was. His mother had believed that Jake's overdeveloped sense of responsibility was what made him so miserable. He'd feel responsible for his son even if he didn't feel any love. No sense giving the guy a heart attack.

Right now, Jamie had better get out to Louisa's. He'd promised to build a snowman at her house today, and even if he couldn't, they'd be expecting him. He drove back the way he'd come, feeling pretty good again until he passed the huge ice heart. The letters were easily legible, etched dark below the opalescent sunlit surface. Had she heard about it yet? Passed it on the way to church? Been teased? Suppose she was so angry at him she never wanted to see him again! He couldn't stand that, not now when he needed her more than ever.

He skidded the car to a stop on the ice of her graveled driveway and dashed into the house through the unlocked storm door calling her name.

"Hi, Jamie," she said and hung the dishtowel in her hand

119

on the back of a chair. May was sitting on a high stool putting the dishes in the closet. "We just finished Sunday dinner, and the folks took the boys over to the mall to buy sneakers. Have you eaten?"

"Are you mad at me?" he asked.

"What about?"

"Then you didn't see it?"

"I've been getting phone calls about it since yesterday. This morning we drove past it after church."

"The whole family?"

"Almost."

He wanted to ask if her parents thought he was a fool but didn't for fear she'd say yes. He waited to hear what her reaction to the heart had been.

"Jamie," she said soberly, "when I said I was fond of you, did you get the idea—"

"No. I knew what you meant. It's just— It was just a joke. I wanted to surprise you with something unusual, and I got a little carried away. You're really not mad at me?"

"Oh, Jamie," she said and put her arms around him and hugged him. "How could I be mad at you? I love you, too, but not that way. I'm just glad you do understand. I feel so guilty. I wouldn't want to hurt you for the world. . . . You realize that everybody knows Vince and I are a couple; so you'll get a lot of flak in school."

"Yeah, well, it won't bother me, just so long as you're not mad. What a relief! I started worrying that I'd made trouble for you with Vince."

"You did," May piped up for the first time.

"What'd he say?" Jamie asked May.

"He told Louisa—"

"It's okay," Louisa interrupted her. "If Vince can't trust me, and if he doesn't understand the difference between kinds of love, that's his tough luck."

"You had another fight with him," Jamie said, and meant it when he added, "I'm sorry. I really am."

"All they do is fight, anyway," May said.

"It wasn't a fight. I just had to make him understand that he doesn't own me and that he can't dictate who my friends should be. No matter what anyone says, I think your valentine is beautiful. It made me feel very special, Jamie."

"Wow! You're welcome." He was so thrilled that he almost forgot to tell her that he had moved out of his father's house.

He got to it later when they were on the frozen pond supporting May between them while she tried to learn to skate on Louisa's old ice skates.

"It's impossible for feet to make right angles like that," Jamie observed as he looked at May's bent ankles.

"Mine can," May said.

"You're not trying," Louisa said. "Slide forward instead of back. You won't fall. We're holding onto you."

"I told you I'd never be an ice skater," May wailed.

"You always say that about anything physical. Didn't you learn to swim when you said you couldn't?"

"But swimming is like reading. You can do it lying down," May said.

"Let's give the kid a rest," Jamie suggested. They struggled to the tree trunk bench at the side of the pond. May loosened her skate laces and rubbed her sore ankles. While they waited for her to recover, Louisa asked Jamie what his father had said about the ice heart.

121

"What made you think of him?" Jamie asked.

"I don't know. Did he notice it yet?"

"Sort of . . . . He called me a jackass."

"That figures," Louisa said, and smiled.

"It wasn't too funny," Jamie said. "As a matter of fact, he made me so mad I moved out on him."

Louisa looked shocked. "Jamie, you didn't! That's terrible."

"Do *you* think I'm a fool?"

"Sometimes you're a little crazy, but in a nice way." She patted his hand comfortingly.

"Thanks," he said. "I'm glad to know you think I'm a nice nut."

"So where did you move to?" May asked.

"The YMCA temporarily. Tomorrow I'm going to look for a night job so I can go to school days. Don't worry, Louisa. I don't plan to drop out."

"What I don't understand," Louisa said, "is that your father's called you down before and you never got that angry with him."

"The time has come, that's all. I've got to prove I'm mature enough to stand on my own two feet. It's a matter of pride."

"Well, I'm not sure you're doing the right thing," she said, "but I have to say you've got a lot of courage."

"I'm doing the right thing. Believe me."

"What kind of a job are you going to get, Jamie?" May asked.

"Don't know. Factory worker, dishwasher, security guard—something glamorous like that."

"You could work at McDonald's," May said.

"Now that's not a bad idea!"

"Did you look through the want ads this morning?" Louisa asked.

"Haven't had a chance. Dad gets the *Times*, but that wouldn't help me, anyway. Do you have a local paper?"

They made a project of it, all three of them. Each one took a section of the want ads and inked around the item that seemed possible. Jamie was a little discouraged to find that even the least appealing work seemed to require past experience.

He had planned to treat himself to dinner in one of the Italian places on Van Vranken near the Y, but Louisa insisted on feeding the poor runaway with leftovers. Then he hung around to play a few games of Atari with Jeff and Billy. He wasn't in any hurry to return to the anonymous room he'd rented.

When he finally headed back downtown, he stopped at a gas station to fill up and to make the phone call to his father. Jake's reaction to his announcement that he'd moved into the Y and planned to become self-supporting depressed Jamie so much that he stopped off at an arcade and tried some of the new games. He lost several dollars worth of quarters in an attempt to erase what his father had said. "Okay, if that's the way you want it. You know where to get in touch with me if you need anything." End of response. Period. End of conversation. Jamie couldn't understand it, and then after a while, he did. Jake was relieved to be rid of him. Jamie's satellite exploded in the blackness of space and the colored lights faded from the screen. It didn't matter. It was just a game, nothing to do with how his life was going, nothing to do with it at all.

⁌11⁌

Jamie took Monday off from school and mapped out his job-hunting strategy while eating soggy pancakes at a closet-sized luncheonette. Answer ads first; then use whatever time he had left to apply at likely places.

The only job that had seemed worth trying for in Sunday's classified section was: "Salesman, no experience, make your own hours, need friendly personality and car." Jamie called and was told to come for an interview at ten. "Novelty items," was all the man on the phone said when Jamie asked what he was to sell. In the meantime he decided to put in his application at the nearby General Electric manufacturing facility whose hulking buildings, surrounded by acres of parking lots, spread farther than the eye could see. Surely the biggest industry in town would have some kind of work for him.

At the gatehouse, past the main entrance, he got directions to the employment office, where an attractive young woman told him they weren't hiring at present, but he could leave his application on file.

"Hey, listen," he said, "I'm willing to do any kind of work at all. You must have something."

"Are you a high school graduate?" she asked, looking unimpressed by his determination. To Jamie's dismay, as soon as he admitted he hadn't graduated yet, she withdrew the form she'd extended to him and said coldly, "We have so many people on layoff waiting to be hired back. You don't have a chance without a high school diploma and experience."

At ten of ten, Jamie climbed two flights of stairs in a decaying building to apply for the novelty sales job. The dirty, glass-windowed door with a handmade sign pasted inside it looked unpromising. The man behind the desk took one look at Jamie and said, "You're too young, kid. I don't care how old you say you are, you'd look too young to our customers." Jamie never did find out what the novelty items were.

On the way back downtown, he tried his luck at a busy auto body repair shop but was told that if he didn't have the skills already, he wouldn't be worth training. "Besides," the young, shirtsleeved manager said, "you got to speak Italian to fit in here."

"I learn fast," Jamie said.

"Go back to school, kid. Education's still where it's at," the young man advised.

McDonald's wasn't hiring, but they allowed Jamie to fill out an application at least. None of the three restaurants he walked into needed busboys or dishwashers. By dinnertime, he was anxious and tired, also hungry, since he'd neglected to eat lunch.

He got into his car and headed for Louisa's to renew his optimism by pouring his experiences into her sympathetic ear. Job hunting was a demoralizing experience. On the way, he drove past his ice valentine, which was doing fine in the ten-degree weather.

A car turning into the condo complex tooted its horn at him. Jamie recognized the rust-fringed gas hog Maury drove. Zingo! Hadn't Maury said he was planning to leave his job soon? And he was on duty evenings and weekends, wasn't he?

Jamie made an illegal U turn and charged into the condo complex and over to the tennis club. He parked and sprinted inside. Maury was just hanging his jacket on the rack near the entry.

"You still leaving this job, Maury?" Jamie asked urgently.

"Shush," Maury said and looked nervously around to see who was listening. Nobody was. He stood close to Jamie to say, "I didn't tell them yet. I'm gonna quit without giving notice to show the bastards. They think they can screw me out of a night's pay just because the receipts didn't add up right once, but I'll show them. Soon as I get this week's paycheck, I'm gone. Just gone." Maury shot his hand wide to show the speed of his exit.

"Then is it okay if I apply for your job, so long as I don't let on you're leaving?" Jamie said.

"How you going to do that?"

"I'll just say I want work here, and if they ever get an opening, would they give me a chance."

"You could do that, yeah," Maury said. "Be my guest."

Jamie slapped his benefactor on the arm and walked briskly toward the manager's office. Luckily Mr. Fazio was there.

Jamie gave him a big grin and a hearty greeting. The elderly manager knew Jamie as the son of a paying club member as well as an occasional part-time employee, so a certain geniality showed in his manner toward Jamie.

"Listen," Mr. Fazio said after Jamie stated his business, "I'd give you the desk job nights in a minute if I didn't have that kid out there already. He's got his head screwed on funny, I don't mind telling you. Careless as all get out."

"Well, if he ever quits—"

"Or gets fired. Yeah, I'll keep you in mind. Your father think it's okay, you working nights while you got school still?"

"Oh, sure. He's a great believer in working hard, and so am I."

"Well, if I need you, I know where to find you."

Jamie gulped. Should he admit he was living at the Y now? No way would Mr. Fazio risk getting between father and son, especially when the father was a club member.

"Maybe I'll just check in with you every so often," Jamie said. "I'm kind of hard to reach." Then he had an idea. "Or you could reach me at my friend's house. There's always someone home there." He waited while Mr. Fazio wrote down Louisa's number.

"Murphy," Fazio said. "Is that Dr. Murphy plays racquet ball Tuesday nights?"

"No, no," Jamie said. "This is a girl I know from school. They don't belong to the club."

"A girl? Say, was that *you* did that ice thing out there by the road? 'Jamie loves Louise.' Pretty cute. That was *you*, then?" He chuckled.

"Yeah, that was me," Jamie said, and blushed and shrugged.

127

"Well"—Fazio kept laughing—"if that girlfriend of yours don't appreciate what you did, she don't know nothing. That was something, telling the world right out how you felt about her. Really cute."

"Yeah, well—" Jamie tried to think of something to say that would undo whatever damage being "cute" had done him in Mr. Fazio's eyes. "It was just a joke, kind of silly, but I thought she'd get a kick out of it." To disassociate himself even further from foolishness, he waxed businesslike and ascertained that the job, if he got it, paid minimum wage and was five to midnight on six days of the week, although the hours varied over weekends.

"Yeah," Mr. Fazio said with a final reminiscent chuckle, "it's great to be young."

Jamie left the clubhouse confident he'd get the job. His luck had turned. He could feel it.

The Murphy family was assembled at the dinner table when Jamie walked into the kitchen. He was apologizing for intruding when Mrs. Murphy said, "Sit down and eat with us, Jamie. It's just Sloppy Joes, but there's plenty of it." She gestured at an empty space with one birdlike hand. It seemed impossible to Jamie that anyone so small could have had six children.

Jamie looked at Louisa for permission. She seemed to hesitate, then said, "Sit down. I'll get you a plate."

Happily, he sat on the other end of the picnic bench that served Jeff as a chair since he'd broken his regular one by falling down the basement stairs with it. Jeff had come out unscathed, but the chair was laid up for repairs. "The kids at school were all talking about you," Jeff said.

"Middle school?" Jamie asked with surprise.

"Well, they didn't know who you were, but they all thought that heart thing was weird."

"The girls didn't," May protested. "The girls thought it was cute."

"Cute!" Jamie repeated. The word was beginning to make him slightly nauseous.

"I predict you started a tradition with that heart, an annual attempt to express one's sentiments in snow sculpture," Mr. Murphy said. His eyes twinkled mischievously in his broad face as he forked up more of his Sloppy Joe. "Next year they'll be trying to outdo you," he said between mouthfuls.

"I'm the only one who hasn't seen it yet," Mrs. Murphy said. "I'll have to make it my business to drive by before it melts."

"Oh, it'll be there for a while," Mr. Murphy said. "Unless Louisa's fellow takes an ax to it." He laughed. Like Mr. Fazio, he seemed to find Jamie's gesture hilarious.

"Vince still mad?" Jamie asked.

"He won't believe Louisa's not encouraging you," May said.

"I think this public exchange of my private business has gone far enough," Louisa said. She served Jamie a steaming mound of savory hamburger meat over two thick slices of bakery bread.

Jamie was so hungry that his mouth watered, but before he picked up knife and fork, he apologized. "I'm sorry, Louisa. I hate to cause you trouble." He waited to hear her answer before beginning to fill the painful hole in his stomach.

"Publicly conveying your affections is an act of courage in

129

today's disaffected society," Mr. Murphy said. "That ice heart took guts, Jamie. You don't have to apologize for it."

"Vince will recover, I'm sure," Mrs. Murphy said.

"Half the girls in the high school said they wished Jamie'd built it for them. Didn't you say that, Lou?" May asked.

Jamie smiled at May gratefully. Too bad she wasn't a few years older. What an advocate he had in that kid!

"Eat, Jamie," Louisa said. "We'll talk about it in private after dinner."

The conversation turned to Billy, who had gotten in trouble with his gym teacher for forgetting his sneakers for the second time in a row. He claimed some kid had swiped them.

"That was the second pair of new sneakers this month," Mr. Murphy complained.

"If they got swiped, it wasn't his fault," Jeff defended his brother.

Jamie had seconds and offered to do the dishes, but May said it was Jeff and Billy's turn and they shouldn't be allowed to get out of it again.

"I'd like to speak to Jamie privately now, anyway," Louisa said. "I have to make a million phone calls tonight for the Valentine dance. Can we be excused, please?"

"Certainly," Mrs. Murphy said.

Louisa led Jamie upstairs to her room, explaining, as she shut the door behind them, that otherwise they'd have May hanging around to put her two cents in. Jamie blinked at the pink and lavender ruffled bedspread and curtains, the costumed doll collection, the sheer daintiness of Louisa's personal environment.

"I didn't know you liked ruffles that much," he said, touched by this revelation of Louisa's inner self.

130

"Then you don't know me very well," she said.

"You sure don't dress the way this room looks."

"I don't like looking foolish." There was a double meaning in the way she said the words and the intent way she was looking at him.

"You changed your mind, huh?" he said. "About the ice heart?"

"Everybody in school keeps asking me whether I'm still going with Vince or if I'm seeing you now. I don't know how to answer them without making you look like—"

"A jackass," he supplied. "That's what my father called me."

"And I'm beginning to sympathize with Vince, frankly. I'm sorry, Jamie, but it's turned out to be a disaster for us both." She sat down on the edge of her bed. He remained standing, an elbow on her dresser top where a pink brush and comb rested beside a mirror with hearts around its lacquered frame. "I'm mad at Vince for not trusting me," she continued, "but he's got good reason to be upset with the whole school making dumb remarks to him. This thing's gotten so out of hand!"

"Hey," he said. "I'll make a public announcement that you and I are just friends, and that you've never led me to believe otherwise. How's that? Or I could write him a letter."

"No," she said. "You don't have to confirm what I've already told him. However bad it looks, he should believe me. If he really respects me, he'll come around." She sighed. "Maybe we'll get a warm spell and the heart will melt."

Jamie's flesh-and-blood heart shuddered as he understood for the first time how hopeless his case was. He'd always clung to the belief that someday a miracle would happen, that she would fulfill his daydreams of her and turn to him, not as a friend but as a man. Now, in the camera click of an instant, he knew that she would never see him that way.

"I suppose," she said, "that when Vince and I go to the Valentine dance together, the kids will stop talking. We just have to get through this week, that's all."

He apologized again, and again she absolved him. "Okay," she said, "let's forget it now. Tell me how your job hunting went."

Briefly, he told her about giving her number to Mr. Fazio and his expectation of a job opening at the club. "I don't want Fazio to know I've left home," Jamie said. "He'll think it's bad business for him to give me a job then, sort of like being on the wrong side of a war."

"I don't know," she murmured. "Maybe you shouldn't have left home. After all, your father is your only close relation, and you've lived with him your whole life and put up with his ways this long. It's only a few months until you finish high school. It would make a lot more sense to move out then, if you feel you have to."

"Boy, you sure have done an about-face on everything. Yesterday you understood that I need to be treated with a little respect for a change."

"But the ice heart *was* foolish, Jamie," she said. "I didn't want to hurt your feelings by saying so yesterday, but—"

"But now you care what people say. What's happened to you? You're not the bold kid you were in fourth grade."

"Oh, Jamie, I know it," she cried. "In fourth grade I was sure I could figure out the right answer to everything, but the older I get the more confused I am."

132

She looked so unhappy that Jamie took pity on her. "Hey, cheer up. Like you said, we just have to get through this week, and after all, I'm the one with egg on my face, not you."

"And your father? You won't give him another chance?"

"I can't," he said simply. His lack of anger seemed to convince her that he knew what he was doing, and she promised to stick by him.

He asked her if she thought her mother would have any leads for him on inexpensive apartments, and Louisa promised to inquire.

"Unless she'd object to encouraging the delinquency of a minor," he said.

"Are you being delinquent?"

"No," he said, "just keeping my ego from breaking into pieces like Humpty Dumpty."

Louisa considered. "You'd better locate a place to live before you start working, or you won't have time to set up housekeeping with school and a job to think about." Now that she was concentrating on practical matters, she sounded like her old, confident self.

It pleased him that she was willing to help him despite her doubts. He had to be satisfied with that and stifle his urge to pull her into his arms and kiss her. That would just convince her they couldn't even be friends, and however bittersweet their relationship was, it was better than none at all.

◂12▸

JAMIE HAD BECOME a celebrity in school. Kids who had never said hello before had a comment for him now when he walked down the hall. Mostly it was razzing. "That was a weird-looking snowman, Jamie." "Too cheap to pay for a valentine card, Landes?" "Here comes the romantic comedy lead himself! Hey, Jamie, did she say yes yet?"

He answered them all with a goodnatured grin, meeting shove for shove and handclasp with handclasp. Not only did he not mind the attention, he secretly enjoyed it. Until Wednesday.

As Jamie approached the crossroads of the school in front of the auditorium after third period Wednesday, he saw Vince Brunelli walking toward him with head bent, listening to a short male companion. Jamie's first impulse was to duck into the library, which was right beside him. His second was to keep going and see what would happen. Their collision course must have looked like a shootout in a Western town to a pair of Louisa's friends because they stopped short to watch. One was Donna, a black girl who had succeeded Louisa as captain of the volleyball team, and the other, a frizzy blonde, was class vice president. Immediately, people bunched around them to see what was going on, even those who didn't know anything about Jamie or his roadside valentine.

Vince played his part instinctively. As soon as he looked up and saw Jamie, his eyes narrowed, his jaw tightened, and his long, thick torso tensed. Jamie stood his ground anyway, determined not to be the first to step aside.

"That was an asshole thing you did," Vince said evenly.

"What was?" Jamie asked.

"That snow thing. You had no right to build it. Louisa's my girl."

"Everybody's got a right to express their feelings."

"She's my girl," Vince repeated through clenched teeth.

"Lucky you," Jamie said.

Vince looked murderous. His fingers squeezed into fists, but when a long minute had passed and Jamie hadn't matched his aggressive stance, Vince made an obvious effort to control himself. He lowered his head and continued walking without changing his course. His arm grazed Jamie's shoulder. The jolt staggered Jamie, who barely managed to regain his balance.

"Asshole," Vince tossed over his shoulder.

"Nice meeting you," Jamie answered and waved genially.

Louisa's friends laughed. The crowd dispersed. Donna's beautiful sloe eyes glowed as she said, "Nice going, Jamie. You didn't give that big mother an inch."

"I didn't?" Jamie asked. It seemed to him he'd come out second best in the shootout.

"Don't tell Louisa on me, Jamie," the frizzy-haired blonde said, "but I hope you beat out Vince. That guy's hung up on male domination. It makes me sick the way she waits on him in the cafeteria, and yesterday, would you believe, he asked her to mend his smelly gym shorts for him."

Jamie grunted, too embarrassed to come up with more comment than that.

"Listen," Donna said. "I hear you're looking for a cheap pad."

"How'd you hear that?"

"Louisa asked me if I knew of anything. There happens to be an unfurnished rental near where I live. The guy who owns it is missing a few marbles, but you could check it out. I'll write down the address."

Jamie thanked her, and while Donna scribbled, he smiled at the blonde, who had changed her name from Millicent to something he couldn't remember offhand. "I appreciate the rooting section," he told her.

When the girls had hurried off to their next class, someone clapped Jamie on the back and punched his arm. "Hey, Wizard, how you doing?" Jamie asked, recognizing his partner from auto mechanics last year.

"Getting by, just getting by," the angular, cross-eyed fellow said. "I drove by your famous testament to love this morning. Didn't know you were such a romantic fella. Congratulations."

The warning bell rang. Wizard walked beside Jamie to study hall. Strange, Jamie thought, that by making himself vulnerable to teasing and attack, he'd finally attracted some comradeship.

After school he called the places he and Louisa had circled in yesterday's paper. Two prospective landladies would not take a single man. Three didn't answer and one apartment was already rented. Tired of sitting in the phone booth, Jamie drove out to the address Donna had given him. Spur-of-the-moment things sometimes worked out best. The house was on the wrong side of the river from Schenectady, close to the railroad tracks, in a commercial zone with a mixture of homes and small businesses—a printing company, a small boat sales shop. He found the number on a mailbox at the edge of a dirt driveway paved with snow and ice. The yard was fragmented with fallen-down sheds and odd-sized outbuildings that gave the place a ramshackle look. On the open front porch, a discarded refrigerator stood beside a pile of chairs, some stacked with legs up, and a carton of wood scraps. Well, he couldn't afford a palace, Jamie thought.

He parked his car and followed a trodden path from the detached garage on the side to the back door. An old man with grizzled cheeks wearing baggy pants and a rakish Greek seaman's cap whipped open the door before Jamie could ring. "What d'ya want?" the old man growled.

"I understand you have an apartment to rent."

"What do you want it for?"

"To live in."

A fat, shaggy dog of indeterminate breed standing beside the man wagged its tail at Jamie. Taking heart from the canine welcome, Jamie tried a smile. After all, the old man could be more fearful than hostile.

"Just you wants the place?" the old man asked.

"Just me." Jamie crouched and whistled to the dog, who wriggled closer and submitted his head for petting. Jamie obliged, although the dog smelled and didn't look too clean.

"You got a job?" came the next question.

"I can pay the rent," Jamie said. "I'll give you a deposit if I like the place—after you let me see it."

In silence the old man studied him. "Can't trust nobody nowadays. . . ," he grumbled. "Well, I'll show it to you. It's up over the garage. Wait here a second till I find the key."

The dog followed the old man inside. Jamie waited a good five minutes before his prospective landlord returned wearing a heavy wool shirt and a more amiable expression.

"Halston Amsley's the name," he said, and held out his hand. Jamie shook it and introduced himself.

Halston Amsley led Jamie into the detached garage through a door alongside the overhead one and up a flight of dark stairs. "Wood stove in the bedroom heats it in winter, but there's plenty of wood in the pile. Nothing to worry about that. You just gotta watch the dampers and remember to feed it." He opened the door at the top of the stairs and let Jamie in ahead of him. The apartment looked clean and included a small living room, bedroom, kitchen and a bathroom with a junior-sized tub, sink and toilet. The walls were papered in garish floral patterns.

"Finished this place off for the wife's mother, but she and the wife both died on me in the same year. Now I live alone. Sell some firewood; don't do much else. . . . Like it?"

"How much?" Jamie asked.

"Oh, I don't know." The old man turned suddenly shy.

138

"What can you afford? It's been empty a while. Two hundred too much?"

"I'm only earning minimum wage," Jamie said, not sure what he could and could not afford.

"Well, you got to pay your own electricity. Water and heat is included and you got a nice view of the fields from the kitchen window. I guess I could take a hundred and fifty if you give me a couple of months in advance."

"Sold," Jamie said and held out his hand for another shake.

"When do you plan on moving in?" the old man asked.

"Soon as I get some furniture," Jamie said.

He drove back to the Y and called Louisa. He would have driven directly to her house, but he didn't want to make things harder for her by bumping into Vince again. She might just decide their friendship had become too costly.

"Guess what," he said when she answered the phone. "Your girlfriend Donna found me an apartment."

"Excellent," she said. "Furnished?"

"Not yet. But all I need is a mattress and maybe a table and chair."

"No way!" she said. "That'd be too depressing. You have to make it home with curtains and pictures and scatter rugs and things like that."

"Tell you what," he said. "You come shopping with me Saturday and advise me on how to spend the rest of my bank account."

"Did you get a job yet?"

"No, but I will."

"You hope," she said. "Well, Saturday night is the Valentine's Day dance, and I've got to get there early to help set up, but I guess I could go to the Salvation Army Thrift Shop and a couple of the used furniture places with you during the day."

"The Salvation Army *Thrift* Shop? What kind of adviser are you?" he asked her in mock horror.

"All the most elegant first apartments in town come from the thrift shop," she informed him. "Or else from garage sales. For garage sales, we'll have to—"

"Check the newspaper," he finished for her. "You've got me hooked on the classified section already, Louisa."

"This should be a fun project," she said.

He hesitated, then asked cautiously, "How's it going with Vince?"

Her voice turned cautious, too. "He told me he tried to have it out with you in school today, but you wouldn't fight. He's still convinced you're his rival."

"I only wish he was right."

"Oh, Jamie."

"Anyway, if you're still going to the dance with him, I guess our friendship hasn't caused you any serious trouble after all."

"Actually," she said, "it's forcing me to straighten out a few things with Vince. Listen, don't worry. Vince and I have a solid relationship."

While he swallowed that bad medicine, Louisa went on to tell him about May getting in trouble in English for using bad language in a composition. May had been indignant when her teacher told her to change it, arguing that it was part of the dialogue and she wasn't responsible for what her characters said.

"She was so furious," Louisa said, "that she announced she wasn't going to school anymore. Dad had an awful time getting her to understand the teacher's position. Of course, the fact that he was laughing all the while didn't help."

"You've got a wonderful family," Jamie said.

"Which reminds me," she said, "have you called your father and given him your new address?"

"Give me a break. I only just got it," he said.

So he had a date with her Saturday, he thought as he hung up. Or a kind of date, anyway. Who knew? If he was really lucky, Vince might come down with the flu or break a leg, and then she'd need another escort for the dance. He imagined walking into the high school gym with Louisa on his arm. "Guess your ice heart worked," they'd say, and he'd just grin and look cool. Louisa! She was too strong minded to kowtow to a heavyweight like Vince for long. What she really needed was someone who would let her grow and flourish, someone who would appreciate her as she was, someone like himself.

He called his father to let Jake know all was well. Until the job was secured, the new address had best remain secret.

"Where the devil are you?" his father wanted to know.

"I'm okay, Dad. Just wanted to tell you not to worry about me." He avoided Jake's questions, simply repeating assurances that he was doing fine and would be in touch when things were more settled. "In fact, you'll probably see me sooner than you think," Jamie said. He imagined his father walking into the tennis club one night and finding Jamie behind the desk. Patiently, he listened to Jake's labored explanations of why he needed to know where Jamie was and how

141

unreasonable it was to be incommunicado. "You can always get hold of me in school, Dad."

Silence. "You're still going to school?"

"Well, sure. What'd you think? I want to graduate this June."

"Good," his father said. "I was afraid you'd dropped out."

"Well, I haven't. . . . Everything okay with you?"

"Fine . . . . Jamie, I don't see the necessity of maintaining separate residences. I'm not home enough to get in your way much."

"Yeah," Jamie said. "Well, it's hard to explain."

"I want you to come home," Jake said.

"I've got to manage on my own for a while, Dad."

"I don't see what you're in such a rush about. You'll be on your own soon enough, next year when you're in college."

"Yeah, well, I'll be in touch." Before his father could argue, Jamie put the receiver down. Then he fumbled for another dime and dialed the tennis club. Maury answered and was noncommital about how things were going.

Afterward, Jamie felt anxious. Suppose he didn't get a job at the club? Suppose he didn't get any kind of work and had to crawl back home to his father? Humiliating. Tomorrow, after school, he'd better start job hunting again.

◄13►

JAMIE WAS SO EAGER to get out of the faceless room at the Y that he bought a mattress and boxspring through an ad in the paper, tied it to his car roof and moved into his new apartment with it Friday night. His sleeping bag did as a blanket, and the discount house provided all his linen needs. It gave him satisfaction to slit open the plastic and make up his own bed in his own home with printed sheets so gaudy they brightened up the whole room. The wood stove intrigued him, and he spent a lot of time fussing with it, learning to control the combustion process to keep as much of the apartment as warm as possible without making it so hot he had to open the bedroom window.

Saturday morning, Valentine's Day, Jamie looked outside. The weather had remained at a glum, subzero impasse with threatening skies that never delivered the snow they promised. He breakfasted from a package of doughnuts and water from his kitchen sink and took off to pick up Louisa for the big shopping excursion.

He was tempted to stop at the tennis club and check about the job again but didn't want to risk encountering his father. Also, giving Mr. Fazio the idea he was overanxious might have a negative effect. Neither the hospital nor the supermarket he'd applied to for afterschool work had encouraged him, and he suspected the applications he'd filled out had gone in the wastebasket. Still, no point getting desperate until the last penny was gone from his bank account. Of course, that might be today. He had told Louisa what he had to spend, and she'd promised to make him a list of housekeeping essentials.

The sky was opaque milkglass shading into gray. Dark tree trunks wrote an indecipherable language against the frozen landscape. Tonight Louisa was going to the Valentine's Day dance with Vince. All right, but today she was his and there was no point in seeing gloomy tidings in the weather. Jamie smiled as he pulled into her driveway and walked into the Murphy kitchen.

May came running. "Jamie, can I come, too? Louisa said I could if you don't mind."

"Sure," he said, hoping his disappointment at not having Louisa to himself didn't show. He didn't want to hurt May's feelings.

"She'll be down in a minute," May said. "She's trying on the dress she's going to wear tonight. You're lucky Mother's out. She was going to have a talk with you."

"About what?"

"Well, she doesn't think you should've moved out on your

144

father. She says fighting with your father is normal at your age and that he probably feels worse about it than you, but men never know how to talk to each other. She says you ought to be patient with him because he works under pressure all the time."

"You're right. I'm lucky she's not home. What did Louisa say?"

"Oh, Louisa defended you. She said you knew what you were doing."

"May," Louisa said walking into the kitchen, "you're a regular little tape recorder. Isn't there anything you hear that you don't repeat?"

"Well, you don't think we should be talking about Jamie behind his back, do you?" May demanded.

Louisa hung a dress over the back of a chair. "I'll have to iron this later."

"That's the dress you're wearing for the dance?" he asked, and when she nodded, looking embarrassed, he said, "It's pretty."

"At least it makes me look thin," Louisa said. She looked wonderful to Jamie in jeans and a white sweater, her cheeks flushed and her eyes bright. "That man at the tennis club called an hour ago," she told Jamie. "He wants you to start work tomorrow."

"Hallelujah!" Jamie shouted. He grabbed May and swung her around in a circle.

"Put me down," she screamed. "I throw up when I get dizzy."

He put May down and said, "Let's go. Now I can spend every penny in my account. We can buy out the town."

"I *thought* you'd be pleased," Louisa said, smiling.

In the car, Louisa presented him with two lists. On one were all the names and addresses of used furniture stores and weekend garage sales. On the other were the items she thought he needed to buy.

May leaned over the back seat and squeezed Jamie in a half-embrace, half-wrestling hold. "This is going to be such fun," she said. "I adore garage sales."

"Just remember you only have two dollars to spend and don't take forever deciding what you want," Louisa warned her. "Jamie's not going to have any spare time for shopping after today."

"Potholders!" Jamie said at the traffic light where he glanced at the list she'd given him. "A colander—what's a colander?"

"That's May," Louisa said. "I put her in charge of adding kitchen necessities. You don't need a colander."

"It's to wash vegetables in," May said. "And you don't need potholders, either, because I'm making you some as a house-warming present."

"Thanks." Jamie dropped the list as the light changed. "I wouldn't want to go broke buying potholders."

Their first stop was a garage sale at a small house just across the bridge into town. Folding tables in the garage held several families' collections of cast-off bric-a-brac and used clothing and small appliances in dubious condition. May was attracted to a china-headed doll with a chipped nose which she examined while Louisa tried to find practical items for Jamie. He discovered a table-sized soccer game which was played with small figures on metal rods and was only missing a Ping-Pong ball to be usable.

146

"What do you need that for?" Louisa asked when he dragged it to the card table where a girl May's age was acting as cashier.

"It's a bargain," Jamie said. "For two bucks I can entertain all my guests."

Louisa showed him an imitation brass lamp in good condition, but Jamie said it was too conservative.

"Conservative?" she said. "What kind of stuff are you looking for?"

"Things with style, with character. The opposite of YMCA anonymous."

"You're going to have to show me what you mean," Louisa said as she eyed the table-sized soccer game. Jamie just grinned and stowed it in his car trunk.

The Salvation Army Thrift Shop was their next stop. Acres of discarded sofas, chairs and tables crammed the front of the dingy warehouse while clothing racks full of used merchandise and bins of shoes and bags and underwear awaited toward the back. Some items looked so decrepit that Jamie wondered why they hadn't been sent directly to the dump. He and his female scouts skirted a tower of mattresses and boxsprings beyond which Jamie spotted a wine red silk sofa with a double-curved walnut bow framing its stiff back. The elegantly carved and curved sofa struck him as exactly right.

"Here we go," he said. "How's this for style?"

"This? You're kidding," May said. "It's awful."

"It doesn't even look comfortable," Louisa said.

"It's only a little faded and what a steal at fifty bucks!" Jamie said, undismayed by their lack of enthusiasm. "I like it." He sat down on it. Dust puffed up on either side of him.

147

"It's outrageous," May said, as angry as if he were insulting her by his choice.

"You got it. Outrageous will be my style." Jamie crossed his ankle over his knee and leaned back, arms spread wide. "How do I look?"

Louisa laughed. "Outrageous," she said.

"Then we'll take it."

After making sure delivery charges were included in the cost, and paying for the couch, Jamie followed Louisa to a lamp she had found. "Just the thing to go with your couch?" she asked with a mischievous gleam in her eyes. The lamp was grotesque, a ceramic dragon with a long red tongue and a shade of torn silk.

"Oh, ugh!" May made gagging sounds.

"Perfect," Jamie declared, straight faced, and when Louisa protested that she'd only been kidding, he swept up the lamp and paid for that, too. "Now look for something unique to stand it on," he ordered.

This time it was May who located the three-tiered table with fluted edges. It was water stained, but was only ten dollars.

Laughing, they entered a used furniture store on the sleazy street where the trolley line used to run. The street edged the poorest section of town and was lined with bars, adult book stores and car parts places, a laundromat, pizza parlors and used furniture stores. The sturdy-looking dresser which caught Jamie's eye as soon as he entered would have been handsome if the veneer hadn't peeled away from one side.

"Probably stood against a heating duct," Louisa said. "Maybe if you put that side against a wall—"

"We'll take it," Jamie said.

While he negotiated the price with the store owner, he saw May fingering some blue glass beads and bought them for her. "From me to you," he said and presented them to her so ceremoniously she blushed.

"Why are you wasting your money?" Louisa said to him. "May's got her own."

"If I feel like buying my second-best girl a present, why can't I?" he said, and bought Louisa a red velvet pin holder with a china lady in the middle. "As a memento of our shopping tour together," he said as he handed it to her.

"Oh, she's so dainty. I love her," Louisa enthused.

"She looks like you," he said.

"Jamie, don't be ridiculous." Louisa tossed her head, negating the compliment, but she looked pleased, anyway.

While Jamie helped the store owner tie the dresser onto the rack on top of his car, Louisa located some enamel pots in good condition.

"These will be your housewarming present from me," she said.

They stopped for a quick hamburger and milkshake. Time was running out. Louisa allowed they could get in one more garage sale. She was enjoying herself, Jamie was glad to see. He suggested the girls pick out a set of dishes for four and eating utensils while he looked around the houseful of items on sale for a kitchen table.

"Couldn't you get *some* stuff from your father's place?" Louisa asked.

"No way. This is strictly my own operation," Jamie said. He found a small, bright yellow formica table and a pair of wooden folding chairs that he could use with it. The pleasant woman in charge of the sale said she'd hold the table and chairs for him, and he could pick them up tomorrow. His car was already full.

Louisa and May proudly showed him their dish selection. "See, the plates are from a different set, but don't they look nice with the cups and saucers, Jamie?" May said.

"Too nice. They hardly fit my decor."

"Well, you don't want to overdo it," Louisa said smiling.

"Outrageous can't be overdone," he said, but he bought the dishes and allowed the girls to talk him into a spatula which Louisa informed him he couldn't cook without.

"I've been cooking for years without a spatula," he said.

"You need it to turn over your eggs," May told him.

"I don't make eggs."

"But you might," May said, and Jamie granted her that possibility.

"I really have to get home. I'm later than I thought I'd be already," Louisa said regretfully.

He immediately packed them into the car along with his belongings and headed toward Charlton. He wouldn't even stop to unload the dresser, although Louisa said it would only take a few extra minutes and she wanted to help with it.

"You can see how everything looks when I invite you to my housewarming," he said.

"Do I get invited, too?" May asked.

"Of course you do. Aren't you one of my girls?"

He was feeling so good that when he stopped the car in Louisa's driveway, he turned her face to his and kissed her on the lips without asking her permission. "Happy Valentine's Day and thanks for helping me," he said.

She hadn't resisted his kiss. He had taken her by surprise, and now she was quiet as she got out of the car and walked to her house, almost forgetting to wave good-by to him.

"Think I made her mad?" Jamie asked May, who was taking her time extricating herself from the packed back seat.

May shrugged. "How should I know? Personally I'd rather be kissed by you than by Vincent Brunelli anytime."

"I love you, too, May," he called as she skedaddled for the house, embarrassed by what she had said to him.

Still, driving back to his new apartment, he felt the misery settle into his chest. She was going out with Vince. Vince was the one she'd chosen and nothing, not ice valentines or any amount of friendship, would change that. He got the dresser upstairs with the grudging help of his landlord, who disappeared as soon as he'd finished, leaving Jamie with the distinct impression that the next favor he asked for would be refused on principle.

The lamp and table, which Jamie had carried along in the trunk, looked strange alone in the living room with the soccer game standing on its metal legs. The couch would improve things, no doubt, add just the right outlandish touch to make the room look like a set for a drawing-room comedy. That was what he was aiming for, a spoof, a rakish, wicked look. He needed some kind of picture on the wall—something corny like children kissing or a mustachioed man in a derby hat—and to finish everything off, a pair of swagged velvet drapes. He laughed to himself, imagining it. Then he went down to carry up the dishes and kitchen utensils.

On the way back to town to collect his table and chairs,

he treated himself to pizza for dinner. No sense thinking about Louisa and Vincent at the dance. Tomorrow Jamie would have to start work. He'd better get to bed early, but he was tempted to stop off at an arcade and lose himself for a few hours in that dusky netherworld of cacaphonous sounds and lurid lights. Forget the image of Vince and Louisa at the dance in the pleasure of imaginary adventure. But he'd already spent too much. He needed some money left to feed himself until he got his first paycheck. Maybe he should have gone to the dance too, asked someone to be his date, but then he'd have had to watch Louisa looking radiant with Vince's arms around her.

The snow started again as he drove wearily back to his own place with the table and chairs tied onto his roof. February was such a bleak month. Only skiing made it tolerable, and he hadn't gone skiing lately. To his dismay, he found it was just as lonesome to walk into his own apartment as his father's. The furniture should cheer the place up when the rest of it came. He just needed to get used to living alone, that was all.

He banked his fire. With his sleeping bag pulled tightly around himself, he settled into bed. He hoped Louisa wasn't going to be angry at him for that stolen kiss this afternoon. He should never have risked it. The logical voice in his head had said all along that he couldn't force her to love him. Why didn't he listen to his own good advice? Or was it vanity—he just couldn't believe that he, Jamie Raymark Landes, could love with all his heart and not be loved back? Jackass, Jake called him. Probably Jake was right.

Jamie woke at one in the morning and got up to put another chunk of wood in the stove. He stood with his face close to the luminous red coals, absorbing the heat to make himself sleepy again. Would he ever find another woman as wonderful as Louisa to love? Would he ever feel as deeply again? It was depressing to think he'd reached his emotional peak at seventeen and had nothing but valleys to look forward to hereafter.

"Louisa," he said, his voice a sigh in the dark.

‹14›

THAT SUNDAY, his first day on the job full time, Jamie had the two-to-midnight shift. Since he already knew what to do and his additional responsibilities were easy enough, he wasn't worried about anything except that the garrulous Mr. Fazio would probably mention who his new employee was as soon as he bumped into Dr. Landes. Jamie hoped his father's reaction would not be openly negative. If Jake behaved in his usual taciturn way, he might not react publicly at all, which would be the best thing for Jamie. It would work out, Jamie decided, as he drove to Louisa's house to spend the last few hours before he had to go to work.

Morning sunshine had polished the snow-covered tree branches and ground to a rhinestone glitter. In a world so bright, it was natural to feel happy.

May met him at the door and said, "You can't see her now; she's crying."

"About what?" He felt immediate guilt. He shouldn't have

been so bold with her yesterday, or was it still trouble with Vince—but that was his fault, too.

"I can't tell you. She made me promise not to tell anyone. She's in the bathroom."

"Give me a hint, May. Come on."

May sucked in her lips to keep herself silent. He dogged her into the living room through the kitchen where the breakfast dishes were waiting for whoever was responsible for doing them. May flopped lightly onto the floor. An array of Magic Markers, colored papers and scissors was fanned out around her.

"What are you making?" he asked.

"Birthday cards. Everybody in our family has a birthday in February or March except Louisa and Dad."

"Really? My father's birthday's in February, too." Next week, in fact, he remembered.

"You can use my Magic Markers if you want to make him a card."

"Thanks," Jamie said, "but I wasn't planning to send one. I'm mad at him right now. . . . Listen, does it have anything to do with me?"

"Why should she be crying about you? You didn't do anything to her."

"Vince, then?"

May nodded without looking up as she carefully drew a clown.

"She tell you what it was about?"

"I can't tell you," May repeated, but then she burst out, "but I think that Vince is a jerk. I'd never go out with a bully like him. He's always telling Louisa what's wrong with her, and there's nothing wrong with her. She's a superior person."

"Right," Jamie said. "No question."

May subsided and drew a peaked cap on the clown. "Can you draw noses?" she asked.

"Sort of." He squatted beside her and drew a nose on the clown. She approved and directed him to finish the face for her. He gave the clown a woeful expression. "Do you think she really loves him?" Jamie asked.

"I don't know. But she's acting pretty strange. She used to always be in a good mood, but lately she goes up and down like a lady in a soap opera. Then when I ask her what's wrong, she won't answer. She used to tell me her private things, but no more."

Jamie's optimism disintegrated. "Sure sounds as if she loves him." He lay down on the floor alongside May and started drawing a cartoon of a jackass.

"I wish he'd choke on a fishbone," May said viciously.

"We must wish no ill, even to our enemy," Jamie intoned as if he were a preacher. "You ought to go to church more often."

"But you should hear him," May said. "He doesn't like my sister's voice. It's too loud. He doesn't like the way she tells people what they should do. He says she's too bossy. He doesn't like her clothes or her friends or anything, and I *know* he hates me." May rolled her eyes tragically.

"Louisa must really be nuts about him to put up with all that."

"Oh, she'll tell him off. Like last night—"

"May, you are the worst blabbermouth in the whole world," Louisa said. Her reprimand lacked its usual punch. To Jamie, she appeared pathetic as she leaned against the doorway, looking down at them.

"You feeling okay?" he asked her.

"Not very. What are you drawing, Jamie?"

He handed up the cartoon of the jackass which now had a balloon coming out of its mouth saying, "Happy birthday, Dad."

"You've got talent," she said, "but I hope you're not planning to send that."

Jamie grunted. They both had their troubles. "Listen, I came by to invite you to my place for dinner."

"I'd like to, but I can't," Louisa said.

"Can't when? I haven't even named a date yet."

"Can't, just can't at all." Her lip trembled as if she were close to tears. This was not the vibrant Louisa he knew and admired.

"You get an ultimatum about me from Vince? Has he forbidden you to see me? Is that it?"

"He's giving her a hard time about everything," May said.

"May, will you quit butting into my life?" Louisa drew her shoulders up in a gesture of self-disgust as soon as she finished speaking, and she said immediately, "I'm sorry. I'm not fit for human company today. I'd be better off with Mr. Kwallek's goat."

"He doesn't love you, but we do," May said.

"Oh, May!" Louisa got down on her knees and hugged her little sister tearfully.

Jamie got to his feet. "Well," he said, "I better get going or I'll be late for work. Is it okay if I call you once in a while, or does Vince monitor your phone calls, too?"

"Don't talk like that," she said. "You're my friend, no matter what. You can call and come by whenever you feel like it."

"Whew, I thought our relationship was done for," he said. "Hey, would it help to bring Vince to my party with you?"

"The person you should invite is your father," Louisa said, sounding like her old self again.

"You could make a birthday party for your father," May suggested. "Jamie's father's birthday is in February, too," she told Louisa.

"You should," Louisa said. "You made your point by moving out, Jamie. Now you ought to start making up."

"No way. I didn't move out of his house to have him come and put me down in mine."

"I bet he's hurting," Louisa said.

"Jake doesn't hurt. He's a healer. He doesn't have personal feelings." She had a fairy godmother complex, he thought, always wanting to fix other people's lives. "Don't worry about me," he told her. "You've got your own problems right now."

"It just seems as if one of us could be happy," Louisa said.

"Tell you what, you make up with Vince, and I'll call my father and see if he can be civil over the phone long enough for me to invite him to dinner."

"It's a deal," Louisa said.

May followed Jamie to the back door and whispered, "I thought you loved Louisa. Why do you keep pushing her at the Bozo?"

"Because I love her," Jamie said. He kissed May on the nose and left.

*   *   *   *

158

Jamie was kept busy all Sunday afternoon at the tennis club between phone calls, handling court assignments, charges, checks and cash, plus a freak run on Band-Aids. At two he had a towel crisis when he ran out of clean ones. Then a customer tripped over the vacuum cleaner hose and got mad at Jamie for vacuuming the lobby in the middle of the day.

When he finally got a few minutes free, he called his father. Nobody was home. He tried the hospital and was told the doctor hadn't come in. Jake wasn't signed up for racquet ball, either. Then where was he? It struck Jamie as ironic that he was now worrying about his father's whereabouts instead of the other way around.

Just before his final cleanup work in the locker rooms, Jamie tried the apartment again and Jake answered.

"Hi, Dad. I've been trying to reach you all day. Where the hell were you?" Jamie asked gruffly, in a sly imitation he hoped his father would recognize.

"I went skiing," Jake said mildly. He never had responded to Jamie's attempts at object lessons. Jamie went back to sounding like himself.

"No kidding! Have a good time?"

"Fair."

"Go by yourself?"

"With a friend," Jake said.

Male or female? Jamie was tempted to ask. Instead he said, "Well, I thought I'd give you my new address and tell you where you can reach me if you need me."

"I've got a pen and paper. Go ahead. . . . No phone?" he asked when Jamie had finished.

"I'm not affluent enough to afford a phone," Jamie said.

159

"You can always reach me here at the club—I'm on full time here now, you know—or at school."

"Well," Jake growled, "don't I get to see you at all?"

"As a matter of fact, you're invited for dinner on your birthday if you don't have another commitment." There was silence. "Your birthday's next Sunday, Dad."

"I know."

"Well, can you make it?"

"Yes. . . . That's very . . . . That's nice of you, Jamie." Jake seemed to be having trouble with his throat.

"You getting a cold, Dad?"

"No. . . . Just a minute."

Jamie waited. Jake came back on the line sounding less hoarse. "What should I bring?"

"Nothing," Jamie said. "Come about seven. Okay? I should be able to get the early shift next Sunday."

"If you can't, call my office and let my secretary know. . . . You're doing all right?"

"Sure," Jamie said. "And how about you?"

He listened to the silence of Jake's thoughts. Say you miss me, Jamie thought. Sound as if you love me and I won't even care that you haven't apologized, but all Jake finally said was, "I'm all right, too."

Sunday, Jamie resolved as he hung up, Sunday he'd entertain his father and he'd ask him some of those crucial questions that he'd never had the guts to ask. "Did you feel bad when she died? How did you feel when she left you? Are you sorry I'm your son? Do you love me, Dad?" It was hard to imagine a scenario when those questions really could be voiced. They'd both have to be drunk or awfully mellow or in family therapy or something with a psychologist priming their pumps.

Jamie thought about his mother, how she'd always been the one to explain his father to him. All he knew of Jake's feelings had been filtered through his mother's perceptions, and she hadn't really believed that Jake had a heart.

Jamie could say, "You've got to stop putting me down, Dad. You hurt my feelings when you talk to me like I'm a minus." Then Jake would answer, "I'm sorry; I never realized. It won't happen again, son." Suppose Jamie came right out and said, "I love and admire you, Dad! How do you feel about me?" But Jamie's imagination failed to supply any response to that one.

How old was his father going to be, anyway, on Sunday? Too old to begin a new relationship with his son? Sunday Jamie would find out, if he could get up the courage.

*   *   *   *

May was right. Louisa was acting strangely. Whenever Jamie tried to talk to her that week, she avoided him. In school she was busy, and when he called her, she wouldn't come to the phone. The second time that happened, he asked Jeff, who'd picked up the phone, what was wrong.

"She acts like she's sick, but she claims she isn't," Jeff said. "My mother says to leave her alone and she'll come out of it."

Jamie asked to speak to May then, but all May added was that Louisa was in a bad mood all the time and wouldn't talk to Vince, either.

"You mean, she's not seeing him?"

"Where've you been?" May asked. "They broke up last weekend."

He tried to squelch his rush of pleasure for Louisa's sake, but then forgave himself and let it come. After all, she was better off without a guy who wanted to renovate her personality, and now, at least, there was no impediment to her friendship with him.

He waylaid her in the school cafeteria one lunch period. "Are you still starving yourself?" he asked looking at the anemic hamburger on her tray. "I thought you dumped Bozo."

"Jamie, I don't want to talk about it."

"You're the one who believes talking about it is good therapy."

She winced. "Not yet, please."

"All right, but let me buy you some outrageous dessert to make you feel better—a double chocolate brownie with ice cream and chocolate sauce maybe, or a frozen Milky Way bar, at least."

She closed her eyes, opened them wide and looked at him hard. "Go away and leave me alone, Jamie."

"You don't like me anymore?"

"It's not you I don't like. It's me. I have some soul searching to do."

He yearned to give her a consoling hug. He wanted to offer her his shoulder to cry on, but he knew better than to push her. He left her alone.

That night she called him at the tennis club. "I forgot to ask what happened when you talked to your father."

"How come we can talk about me but not about you? What kind of relationship is this, anyway?" he complained, although it touched him that she should still be concerned about him while she was suffering herself.

"Did I ever claim to be logical?" she said testily. "You have this idea I'm some kind of super organized efficiency freak, but I'm not. Now tell me about your father."

"It went fine," Jamie said. "He's coming for dinner Sunday. Will you come, too?"

"You don't need me."

"Yes, I do. What happens when Dad and I run out of newspaper headlines to discuss?"

"I'm not coming, but May and I will bake you a birthday cake for him. Come by and pick it up anytime that's convenient on Sunday."

"Hey, you don't have to do that!"

"But I want to," she said and hung up on him.

His talk with Louisa on Friday night left him feeling so good that on his way to work Saturday, he pulled into the driveway of a barn that said "Antiques" on its door.

He told the petite, gray-haired woman who answered the summons of the wildly ringing cowbells attached to the barn door, "What I need is a really corny, old-fashioned picture to hang over a far-out couch. It has to be cheap, though."

Her eyes crinkled with pleasure. She helped him pick through dusty pictures in heavy, carved wooden frames and seemed glad to sell him a tarnished and chipped imitation-gold monstrosity for five dollars. The water-stained print behind the glass in the frame showed a young girl with pantalooned legs exposed under her skirts as she reached for the sky in a rope swing attached to the limb of a large tree. Jamie couldn't wait for his father to see it hanging above his bow-backed red silk couch.

163

He was five minutes late for work, but Fazio wasn't there to notice. Luck was going all his way, Jamie thought.

Sunday was hectic. The early shift went from seven until three in the afternoon, and then he had to stop at the twenty-four-hour-a-day supermarket to get steak and salad greens and the ingredients for the clams casino he'd decided on for a gourmet touch. May and Louisa were standing at their kitchen door with the cake wrapped and ready to thrust into his hands when he came to collect it. He'd called them before leaving the club.

"The licorice stethescope was my idea," May said.

"Good luck, Jamie." Louisa blew him a kiss.

He buzzed off, yelling thanks over his shoulder. His stomach was churning more at this coming event than it had over the gymnastics meet.

"Calm down, kid; you'll make it," he told himself as he carried his paper bags, with the cake balanced under his chin, up to his apartment.

The first thing he did was to unwrap the cake and chuckle over the black licorice stethescope with marshmallow ear plugs and diaphragm. Red icing on the white cake said, "Happy birthday, Dad."

Jamie set to work chopping the ingredients for his clams casino. He'd bought a peck of raw clams, but when he tried to pry the shells apart, he couldn't. In desperation, he clattered the resistant shells into a pan, poured water over them and boiled them open. He hoped the cooked clams would taste all right after being baked again with the topping. The cookbook wasn't much help except with the seasonings.

When he looked at the clock, he had only minutes left before Jake's arrival, and the salad still had to be washed and

164

cut up. The housekeeping he'd meant to do would just have to be forgotten. Instead of mixing a dressing, he put a bottle of prepared stuff on the table, with two placemats Louisa had donated and half his collection of dishes. The fat yellow candle he'd bought half price at the supermarket made the table look inviting, he assured himself, as he heard Jake's deliberate tread on the staircase. It was seven. Trust Jake to be prompt.

Jamie took a deep breath, put on a smile and opened his door wide. "Happy birthday, Dad."

Jake proffered a paper wrapped bottle of wine.

"Hey, you didn't have to do that," Jamie said. He unwrapped the bottle. "Excellent," he said. "You'll be happier drinking this than the tomato juice I got."

"We can try both," Jake said amiably.

"Well, welcome to my humble home. I have to apologize; you got short-changed on a present this year because my life savings has gone into toilet paper and pots and pans." Also steak and clams casino, but he tactfully didn't mention that.

"I don't need any presents," Jake said. His eyes made a surreptitious survey of the kitchen.

"The linoleum is pretty crummy," Jamie said, looking at the holes in it, "but for the price, what can you expect?" He hoped his father was also noticing the candle and placemats.

Impulsively, Jamie lit the candle then and there, but the draft from the uninsulated window made the flame wave about dangerously and Jake said, "Maybe you better wait to light it when we eat."

"Sure," Jamie agreed. "So. You ready for the grand tour?"

"Whatever you say," Jake said.

165

At Jamie's suggestion, he shrugged off his sheepskin jacket. Jamie tossed it onto the mattress in his bedroom, embarrassed as he saw he'd forgotten to make up his bed. Naturally, Jake would be standing right behind him, looking in over his shoulder at the bedroom where mattress, dresser and wood stove composed the three-piece suite.

"A little short on housekeeping time this morning," Jamie said. "I had to be at work at seven."

"Where did you get the wood stove?" Jake asked.

"Came with the place," Jamie told him. "The bed and most of my stuff is Salvation Army special. That's the place to find great stuff, Dad. Wait until you see the *pièce de résistance* in the living room."

Jake glanced into the bathroom where a clear plastic drop sheet thrown over the curtain rod had sagged wetly to the floor. Jamie pulled the door shut as he passed and gestured to the living room. "After you."

Jake moved into the middle of the tiny room whose one wall now looked like a stage set for a Victorian comedy. Jamie watched his father's face for a glimmer of amusement, approval, understanding—something. Jake stood in silent astonishment, just staring.

"Wild, isn't it?" Jamie cued him.

Jake nodded, still silent.

"Get that couch," Jamie said uneasily. "Isn't it outrageous?"

For answer Jake eased himself onto the couch, as gingerly as if he expected it to collapse under his weight. Actually, his extra pounds did cause dust Jamie hadn't reached to rise from the cushions on either side of Jake's thighs.

166

"Whoops! Thought I'd taken care of that," Jamie said, and added quickly, "Can I get you something to drink, Dad?"

"You have any Scotch?"

"No, sorry. Just the wine."

"Oh, right. I'll take a glass. Thanks."

In the kitchen Jamie rinsed out two juice glasses. The conversation was about as he'd expected—not what he'd hoped, just what he'd expected. He wondered if he should ask Jake to play the garage sale soccer game, if that would entertain him. "Not likely," he said to himself. Since he didn't have a wine bottle opener, he dug the cork out with a utility knife, crumbling some cork into the bottle. Then he turned on the oven and put in his clams and went back to the living room with a glass of wine and one of tomato juice. His father had lit the dragon lamp. Jake's face was shadowed next to it while the garish green dragon was highlighted, its red fangs gleaming.

"So how did your week go?" Jamie asked, handing over a glass and sitting down cross-legged on the floor at his father's feet.

"The usual, a couple of new patients, nothing remarkable. . . . And how about you? How are you managing with school and a full-time job?"

"Easy. The hours fit perfectly."

"And you're satisfied?"

"Sure."

"It seems to me"—Jake took a gulp of wine and felt his way through what he wanted to say—"that you'd have it a lot easier if you moved back in with me. Whatever I said that offended you, I'm sorry."

167

An apology! Jamie caught it, but it disintegrated in his hands as he realized that it was empty of meaning. Jake had no idea of what he'd done to offend.

"Listen, Dad," Jamie said. "I know I'm a big disappointment to you, and I understand I get on your nerves because we do things differently, but that's just it, see? I don't appreciate being reminded of what a flop I am, and I don't happen to think I'm a jackass." His jaw twitched and his heart beat at an alarming rate as his resentment leaked out. If he was going to talk this way to his father, they wouldn't even make it to the clams casino before Jake walked out.

"Is that what I said?" Jake asked.

"Jackass has been your pet name for me for a while."

"God, I'm sorry!" Jake said and looked as if he meant it. "Your mother used to tell me I had the hide of a rhinoceros. I never wanted to believe her. Certainly to my patients I'm not—but maybe . . . ." He gulped some wine and looked at his shoes.

"More wine?" Jamie asked, to rescue him. It made him uneasy to see his father discomfited. Jamie sipped at his own glass and began making time-filling chatter about the doctors at the tennis club—who was known to management as a deadbeat who never paid bills, who played the roughest game, and who was a sore loser.

Jake listened and finally grunted and said, "Jamie, there's one thing I'm going to insist on. I want you to have a smoke alarm. This place is a firetrap with that wood stove."

"Lots of people live with wood stoves and nobody's house is burning down," Jamie objected, thinking that Jake hadn't changed one iota.

"Old wood houses do burn down. That's what we have fire departments for."

"Faulty wiring can cause fires in new houses."

"Yes, but in old places like this—" Jake persisted.

"Dad!" Feeling his temper rising, Jamie wanted to steer out of this dangerous intersection fast. "I'll get a smoke alarm, okay?"

"And a telephone."

"Hey!"

"I'll pay for it," Jake said. "But I won't have you living in a place where you can't call for help if you need it."

"I better check on those clams," Jamie muttered. Rhinoceros was a good description, and not just the hide.

Jamie checked the oven. It was barely warm. Another dial there he hadn't set, he noted. He sighed, turned it on and returned to his very first house guest.

"So how old are you today?" Jamie asked. "Forty-eight or forty-nine?"

"Fifty," Jake said. He gave his sad, lopsided smile. "Pretty lousy to think that all I've accomplished in half a century is the alienation of my wife and only son."

"I'm not alienated," Jamie said quickly.

"Aren't you? It seems to me I can't open my mouth without getting your back up."

It was beginning to sound as if Jake had come today with a dream of a breakthrough similar to his own. Impulsively, Jamie said, "Dad, could we talk about my mother? Could we really talk to each other?"

Jake's eyes fixed with a frightened intensity on Jamie's face. "You're burning something," he said.

At first Jamie didn't get his meaning. Then he smelled the clams himself. He ran to the kitchen and grabbed May's potholders to rescue the clams. The bread crumbs were a little blackened. He brought in the pan and showed his father. "Think they're still edible?"

"We need some forks," Jake said. They ate in silence. "Not bad," Jake said.

"I wanted to try something special for your birthday."

"I appreciate that, Jamie. . . . So what do you want to know?"

Jamie's hope rose. Jake wasn't avoiding the issue after all. "How you felt after she left and after she died," Jamie said. He watched sympathetically as his father struggled to come up with words.

"Your mother . . . ," Jake said and paused. "I thought she knew how much I loved her. I thought she knew. . . . She was the joy in my life. My work . . . that wasn't all I lived for, like she said, but I have to do it well. I wasn't brought up to shirk duty. You can't put sick people aside and your own pleasure first. I don't think she ever really understood." He sounded regretful. "Or else, I just wasn't enough for her. . . . You asked how I felt after she left? Dead. I felt dead, and if I hadn't had you, I don't know if I could have stood it. You were a good kid, and I knew you—I could see how sad you were when she left, but I couldn't do anything about it, and you proceeded to scare the hell out of me . . . the drugs and then the drinking. She died, and I thought, good riddance. But even so . . . that lightweight musical-comedy fellow she ran off with? . . . I'd always believed she'd see what a mistake she'd made and come back someday. And then she died, and that was the end of that. . . . What had made me so sure she'd come back was I loved her so damned much. Ridiculous, isn't it, to expect that your feelings can force the other person to feel the way you do about them?" Jake cleared his throat and looked at his son with ravaged eyes.

Jamie let his plate clatter to the floor and moved to hug his father, to squeeze against the awful pain in Jake's face. "Hey, Dad, hey," Jamie choked.

Their emotion embarrassed them both. They turned away from each other. Jake pulled out a white linen handkerchief and blew his nose. Jamie wiped his eyes with his sleeve and stood up.

"I better get our steaks cooking," he said.

In the kitchen, he dumped the meat into a pan and put it on the stove. Well, he'd gotten what he wanted. Jake had exposed his soul. So what had his son done in response? He'd ducked out of sight like a coward. A heart-to-heart talk with Jake wasn't as cozy as Jamie had imagined. In fact, it was agonizing, and if Jamie wanted to be fair, it was his turn now. He heard his father in the bathroom and rejoined him when Jake returned to the couch in the living room.

"So," Jake said.

"So don't give up. You're going to get fed yet. It'll just take a few minutes more," Jamie said, and wondered how to introduce the kind of statement he wanted to make.

"One more thing," Jake said. "I suppose I don't have to tell you how much you mean to me, how much I care about you. You know, don't you? I mean, your mother always said I don't have the words, that I'm not capable of expressing feelings. Well, I wasn't brought up to express my feelings. My family didn't consider it necessary or even very civilized. I'm not . . . ." Jake stopped and looked embarrassed, as if he'd already said too much. "What I mean to say is . . . ."

"I love you, too, Dad," Jamie said in a rush. He was overwhelmed that Jake had gone first. "You know I've always been plenty proud to have the greatest doctor in the world for a father."

"Well," Jake said in an attempt at lightness, "let's not exaggerate. Say the second or third greatest." He managed to get both sides of his lips up in a smile this time.

With relief, they went to the kitchen and sat down to their salads.

"Nice salad," Jake said. It was loaded with red onions the way he liked it.

"Wait until you see the cake Louisa baked for you."

"Louisa? Oh, your girlfriend."

"She's just my friend, Dad. I wish she was my girl, but she doesn't think of me that way, unfortunately."

"But she baked the cake?"

"She and her little sister. Her little sister's gone on me. My luck that it isn't the other way around."

"You're young," his father said. "You'll have plenty of girls."

"How about you, Dad?"

"Me? I'm too old for changes."

"You know you're not."

"Then maybe I don't want any."

Jamie sliced the steak. "Look at that, pink inside just the way we like it."

172

"You're a better cook than I am."

"Dad," Jamie said, "I'm still not going to move back in. Not because I don't care about you—I do, a lot—but I've got to be independent for now. Can you buy that?"

Jake shrugged. "Do I have a choice?"

Louisa and May's cake was so good that the two men had seconds. Then Jamie tried to make his father take the rest of it home with him. "It's your birthday cake," he insisted.

"Your girl made it. You keep the rest." They argued and ended by dividing the last half between them.

"How about having dinner with me at the club next week?" Jake asked.

"Sure, that'd be terrific," Jamie said. His answer seemed to cheer Jake up.

"Thanks for the dinner," Jake said, standing at the door with the foil-wrapped cake in his hand. "It was the best party I've had in years."

"Me, too," Jamie said, and slapped his father's arm affectionately.

Jamie was tired but relaxed as he washed up the dishes. It had come out amazingly well. The things Jake had said! All that pent-up emotion all these years. Jake could call him any name he wanted, now that Jamie was sure of his father's true feelings.

In bed that night, Jamie lay mulling over Jake's revelations. What had struck the most sympathetic chord was his father's expectation that his wife would return to him eventually. Hadn't Jamie always comforted himself with the belief that she would either return or call her son to be with her in Jamaica? His bitterness after she died had been the burned-out taste of that dream. It had confused him to feel angry at her for dying. Now he understood why he had. She had cheated both Jake and him by leaving them twice, the last time forever. He and his father had suffered similar bereavements, but Jake's was worse because he had been left finally by both his wife and his son. Jamie felt an upsurge of warmth for his father. Maybe Jamie wasn't the son Jake would have chosen, but nonetheless Jake loved him, always had. And even if the words were never spoken aloud again, Jamie would remember that.

And Louisa? It was time to give up his pursuit. He loved her, but she didn't love him back. Sooner or later she would find another Vince Brunelli, and Jamie was going to have to smile and step back and wish her luck and not try to trip her on the pieces of his broken heart.

*   *   *   *

Later that week Jamie got a letter from his father's lawyer informing him that Jake had deposited substantial funds with the lawyer for Jamie's use, enough to pay for college if he chose to go. All Jamie had to do was submit a request in writing indicating what he planned to spend the money for. Unless the lawyer, who was acting as his unofficial guardian, wanted to question him about it, a check would be issued in his name. "Your father seems to feel you have a need for financial independence right now," the lawyer wrote. Jamie thought the gesture, as complex and unnecessary as it was, was typical of Jake's guarded generosity.

When he joined his father for dinner at the club on Jamie's night off, he thanked him.

"I expect you'll use it wisely," Jake said. "Of course, I'd like to see you go to college, but whatever you do, for God's sake don't go into the furniture business."

"You didn't admire my decorating scheme?" Jamie asked with a smile.

"Let's say it showed more imagination than good taste."

"Shows how little you know, Dad. Wait until you see the spread they're going to do on me in the Sunday supplement some day—bachelor pad of the year is what they'll call it."

Jake laughed. "You could be right," he said. "This world's crazy enough for anything."

Later he proposed that sometime during the summer he and Jamie drive out to Ohio where an uncle and aunt and some cousins from Jake's side of the family lived. "We could do some camping en route," Jake said. "Think you'd want to take off with your father for a couple of weeks?"

"If I can get the time off from my job, that sounds like a great idea, Dad."

They smiled at each other across the table, still trying out the new balance of respect in their relationship but pleased to be in the act together.

◄15►

AT MOMENTS in the weeks that passed during the dismal March when the earth was imprisoned in bitter cold and blue skies rarely showed between threatening clouds, Jamie's courage faltered. He'd come home to his lonely apartment, switch on the lights and stare at the dirty dishes in the sink. Drafts sliced at him meanly so that it seemed colder inside than out. He'd walk into his living room and see it through Jake's eyes as tawdry, really pretty bad.

If it wasn't too late, he'd call Louisa on the phone his father had insisted he have installed. Louisa had come out of her moody period without ever telling him what had been on her mind. All he knew was that she wasn't seeing Vince anymore. Her refusal to confide in Jamie made him question the balance of their friendship. He didn't like always being on the receiving end. On the other hand, he needed her too much to be proud. So he continued calling and reporting to her on the progress of his life. She was the first one he contacted when he got the letter from the college in New Hampshire.

"They want me," he told her. "The crummiest essay I ever wrote and they want me anyway."

"I'm so glad, Jamie," she said. "Now you can head for medical school just like you planned."

"I don't know about becoming a doctor," he said. "I might just try business administration or philosophy or something. You know, break my own trail."

"Excellent," she said. "Good for you."

Louisa didn't have a lot of time to spend with him outside of the phone calls. She had flung herself full tilt into organizing the senior show and was also taking classes toward her Water Safety Instructor Certificate because she planned to work as a counselor during the summer before going off to SUNY in Albany in the fall. Once she surprised Jamie by suggesting that he ought to apply for a job at the camp, too.

"It'd be fun to have a friend there with me," she said. "I don't know anybody except the director."

He was flattered, but didn't take her seriously. She was too independent to need him around, and his summer work at the tennis club was going to include outdoor court maintenance, for which he would get a much-needed raise in pay. He wanted to avoid using the money his father had set aside for him, especially now that he needed it for college.

Early in April, Louisa called Jamie about an invitation to a party she had received. "I really want to go, but everybody's bringing someone. Would you come as my date?"

"Sure would," he said, so jolted with pleasure that he had to warn himself not to start imagining possibilities. It didn't mean anything special. It was just as she said—she needed an escort, and as her good friend, he was the obvious choice.

He maneuvered his schedule at work to have the evening free and set off for the party, anticipating a good time. Louisa acted peculiarly nervous in his car on the way to the friend's house in Schenectady.

"Don't worry. I won't hang around you and cramp your style," he assured her, thinking she might be concerned.

"Don't be silly," she said. "I'm not worried about you." She sat stiffly beside him in a new skirt that she told him she had made.

"I really like that skirt," he said. "You did a good job."

"It makes me look fat," she said. He didn't argue with her. He'd learned he couldn't make her change her mind about herself. Although it was true she had begun to talk about city management as a career possibility, and the last time she called him, she'd said:

"Remember, once you told me you could see me as a state senator?"

"U.S. senator or President was what I said," he amended.

"Well, anyway, I've been thinking. If I could find a man who approved of my career, I could be a wife and mother and senator all at once. Other women have done it."

"You can do anything you want, Louisa."

". . . Because your real friends will be there for you no matter what you become."

"Right," he said. "It's how you feel about yourself that matters most."

"Oh, Jamie, when did you get so wise?"

"Me?" he'd said. "I haven't changed any."

"Then I have," she'd said, and started talking about something inconsequential.

She fidgeted beside him as they crossed the railroad track,
and began chattering about her difficulties in getting cooper-
ation on the senior show production. Too many people who'd
promised chunks of script were not coming through, and often
committee meetings were stymied by no-shows. It was going
to be a disaster, she said. The rush of her words made him
uneasy. Lately he often had the feeling she was using words
to cover up something she didn't want to tell him.

She only stopped chattering when they arrived at the small
brick ranch on a flat, unadorned lot where the party was being
held. It was a modest house, but its entire basement turned
out to be a wood-paneled recreation room as big as the whole
upstairs and equipped with a built-in bar, fireplace and book-
shelves.

Jamie established himself at a Ping-Pong table. By joking
about being unbeatable, he got plenty of challengers and was
tickled when, by sheer luck, he kept winning at a game he
hadn't played in years.

Midway through the evening, Louisa tapped him on the
shoulder and asked if he was ever going to dance with her.

"Soon as I beat out this hot competition," he said, pleased
that she'd asked him. These were her friends. He had thought
she'd be glad not to concern herself with him.

He lost to the girl he was playing against and handed her
his paddle, declaring her the new champion. Then he ambled over to the fireplace end of the room where Louisa was
sitting in a circle of seniors involved in a heated and very
repetitive argument over whether a comedy routine satirizing

the teachers was funny or just plain nasty. Since Jamie wasn't involved in the production, he had no opinion to offer and got bored after a while. He felt like dancing, but rather than drag Louisa away from the discussion, he wandered over to a girl with a left-out look and asked her to dance. He caught Louisa staring at him with an odd expression on her face and wondered if he'd hurt her feelings in some way. He couldn't think how, though, and put it out of his mind.

On the way home, Louisa wanted to know if he'd enjoyed the party.

"Sure," he said. "Did you?"

"It was okay."

"You still brooding about Vince?" he asked with sympathy.

"No," she said curtly and changed the subject. "Tell me about your father. Is the new relationship still going well?"

"Yeah, he's working hard at treating me like a man lately."

"Well, you're acting more like one lately," she said.

"True. At least, I haven't done anything certifiably ridiculous in a while."

He put the handbrake on in the usual spot near her back door. When she didn't move, he thought she might be waiting for some old-fashioned gallantry, so he leaped out of the car and opened the door for her on her side, bowed low and said, "My lady."

She got out slowly, ignoring his hand. "Oh, Jamie!" she said, as if he'd disappointed her, and proceeded to her house, stopping at the door to call over her shoulder, "Thanks for taking me tonight."

"Anytime." He smiled and waved, tolerant of her vagaries.

Accepting life's limitations was his latest definition of maturity. He no longer yearned after more than pure friendship with Louisa. The impossible dreams of his youth had been replaced by sedate adult reality, or so he told himself regretfully.

*　　*　　*　　*

One rainy afternoon in April, Louisa phoned Jamie at the tennis club, where he was covering the desk for a couple of hours to replace an employee who'd gone home sick.

"Could you meet me in Central Park?" she asked. "May's going to a birthday party and I'm supposed to pick her up near there."

"It's still raining," Jamie said. "The park's going to be pretty wet."

"Jamie, I have to see you. A little rain won't hurt us."

"Okay, how about the big kids' playground at five-thirty?"

"I'll be there," she said and hung up.

He wondered at her urgency. What could have made her so anxious? As soon as he could leave, Jamie hurried to the park to find out.

The misting rain increased to a drizzle and diminished again, darkening the late afternoon. Streetlights were lit, and lamps in people's houses. The landscape was ghostly and the empty park had a forlorn look. He parked and waited. All the rain-slicked steel of the play equipment gleamed, and the thrumming of raindrops on his car roof beat a steady background music for the swaying, gray green trees around the dimpled lake.

In a few minutes, Louisa's mother's station wagon drew up

181

next to his car like a steamship putting into port beside a tug. Louisa got out. She wore an unbuckled boy's raincoat and a rainhat tied under the chin and looked as anxious as she'd sounded on the phone.

"How about we do our talking in your luxury liner?" he called out his window.

"It's not raining that hard," she said. "Let's walk."

"Always said I'd do anything for you and that includes getting wet," he said, and got out in his shirtsleeves without a jacket.

The air was warm for April. "Take my arm," Louisa said, producing an umbrella which she opened over his head. "You don't have to get wet."

"So what's the problem?" he asked as they set out, sheltered under the umbrella, across the grass under the trees toward the closed casino where in summer ice cream and popcorn and soda were sold and rowboats were rented.

She studied his face. "Then you really haven't seen this morning's paper, really?"

"Who has time to read newspapers? I'm lucky if I get a second to brush my teeth."

"And no one in school said a word to you?"

"No . . . . What's going on? Someone we know in trouble?"

"No," she said, and looked at the ground. "I wish you'd seen it, though, or someone had told you. Oh, God, I'm so embarrassed! That dumb little sister of mine."

"What'd May do?"

"Nothing. Just talked me into doing something so unlike me I can't believe I did it."

He waited, but she didn't continue. "Want me to start guessing?" he asked. "Tell me when I'm getting hot or cold—"

"No way could you ever guess," she interrupted him. Then she took a deep breath and began again. "May said I ought to be brave the way you were and come right out and tell the world how I felt."

"About what?"

She turned away from him as if she were looking across the lake at the ducks on the far shore. Jamie thought of the ice valentine he'd built. It had melted long ago and he'd given up foolish things. What had she done? "Are you in love again? Not Vince still?"

"Vince?" she said impatiently. "Jamie, you know I stopped seeing him in February."

"Sorry, but how can I tell if you're over it or not? I guess I get a D minus as a mind reader, Louisa."

"I just can't believe nobody in school said anything to you."

"You're stalling." He took her by the arms and backed her up against a tree, umbrella and all. "Out with it, woman. What did you do?"

"I took out an ad in the personal columns," she said. Her eyes were wide as a scared child's.

"An ad for what?"

"Oh, God, I could die!" She refused to meet his eyes. "May said I never risk anything. She said, 'Jamie's not afraid to show the world he cares'—like the snow valentine you built."

"That again! I was crazy to do it when I knew all the while you were Vince's girl."

Now she looked at him sharply. "You mean, you wouldn't do it again?"

"I doubt it. You only get one shot at being that young and

183

foolish." His answer made Louisa groan. "What's the matter?" he asked. "Who are you in love with now?"

"Let me go," she said. "I have to show you something. Someone'll show it to you sooner or later, anyway."

He released her, and she took a scrap of paper from her pocket and shoved it into his hand. It was a newspaper clipping the size of a cigarette wrapper. He stepped under the lighted veil of fine rain from a street lamp and read it. The message went through him like a shot of adrenaline.

"Putting an ad in the paper was all I could think of that was public, and it's your fault anyway. I sent you a million signals and you ignored every one," she complained.

"This . . . this is the greatest thing that's every happened to me," he said. "Louisa, I can't believe it. It's . . . I'm going to frame it. I won!" he exulted.

"You didn't win anything," she said.

"Sure I did." He kissed her, and then kissed her again with all the passion he'd never had permission to show before. She was pliable in his arms at first, and then she began to respond with a strength equal to his own. They swayed together in the rain, dizzy with sensation. Finally Jamie broke away. He had to know.

"How come you changed your mind?"

"I just figured out that the reason I was trying to squeeze myself into the tight little mold Vince wanted me to fit was that I didn't have confidence anyone—any guy—would love me as I am," she said. "I know I'm a big, bossy, hard-headed female, and most boys are scared stiff of women like me. I was so busy trying to make myself over that I didn't even see that *you* liked me as I am. May saw it, but I didn't."

"May's a little genius," Jamie said.

"Maybe. Also, I decided I'm okay the way I am."

"You sure are," he said. "You're the most okay girl in the world." Then he pushed her away and threw his head back and yelled, "She loves me. Louisa loves me."

"Shush," she said. "Are you crazy?"

"Never," he said. "I've been a jackass and a fool, but I won anyway." With a whoop of joy, he ran straight up the rain-slick slide, throwing his arms out wide as he balanced precariously at the top.

"Jamie, you'll hurt yourself," Louisa screamed.

"I can't," he said. "I'm invincible." And he skied down the wet surface of the slide in his sneakers and leaped at the heavy chains holding a swing, clambered up and did a routine from the top bar of the swing stand that would have won him standing ovations at any gymnastics competition.

When he finally rejoined her, panting from his exertions, she was laughing and crying all at once. Wet to the skin, he ducked back under the umbrella to claim another kiss, delicious as rainwater, sweet as triumph, marvelous as the little item she'd had printed in the newspaper for anyone to see: "Louisa loves Jamie."